T0064080

DHAYANAM

DHAYANAM

Kathiresan Ramachanderam

PARTRIDGE
A Penguin Random House Company

Copyright © 2015 by Kathiresan Ramachanderam.

ISBN: Softcover   978-1-4828-4751-2
               eBook   978-1-4828-4750-5

All rights reserved. No part of this book may be used or reproduced by any means, graphic, electronic, or mechanical, including photocopying, recording, taping or by any information storage retrieval system without the written permission of the publisher except in the case of brief quotations embodied in critical articles and reviews.

Because of the dynamic nature of the Internet, any web addresses or links contained in this book may have changed since publication and may no longer be valid. The views expressed in this work are solely those of the author and do not necessarily reflect the views of the publisher, and the publisher hereby disclaims any responsibility for them.

Print information available on the last page.

To order additional copies of this book, contact
Partridge India
000 800 10062 62
orders.india@partridgepublishing.com

www.partridgepublishing.com/india

This book is dedicated to Dyarne who has been the light that has never ceased to shine in my darkest hour, to my mum and dad for their kindness and devotion, to my sis, brother in law and the kids for their endless support and to Cherie, Rudi and Sarah.

PREFACE

There are certain events in one's life that leave a long and lasting impression and many years after the fateful day it continues to play a part in the decisions we make. Like a still frame etched in the mind, the memory joyous or painful, depending on the recipient, and on his or her demeanor, continues to sway a person's judgment and thereafter the person is never the same again. I was the fortunate participant in one such event and years after it continues to have a bearing on the decisions I make. I call it my conscience and it has a name. I call it the spirit soul. It is the pivotal character that altered my perception of life. It was the catalyst that precipitated the change and transformed me from what I was to what I have become.

The spirit soul is always there but is never there, deeply entwined in every sinew of my body, it shackled me to my conscience and try as hard I could, for I resisted for a great many years, I could not break away from the chains that kept me under lock and key, and at a moment's notice, at the very thought of the spirit soul, a kaleidoscope of emotions surface to knock me off balance.

I have never been certain if we were acquainted or it was a figment of my imagination that had somehow come to life. Sometimes I think it is the former and at other times I think it is the latter. I know it exists somewhere in this world, distant and away from me but that is all I know and I know not how to be in touch with it, with the exception of looking deep within myself and there nestled among my fondest memories it shines like an unyielding light.

At times I think it has escaped the clutches of my mind to become a living person and at other times I think it is a figment of my imagination that has somehow transgressed the borders between fantasy and reality. Maybe it is both, real on certain occasions and fictional on others. I am certain that the spirit soul has a form and I am convinced that it can assume any shape or form it wishes. All good things I deduced, all celestial and heavenly beings, all which point us in the right direction, must be equated with the spirit soul.

It can come in any form, in all forms and all sizes. When I was a child I was told that God worked in mysterious ways and that he often assumed the role of a person to do his will. Maybe this was God, in his omnipresent and omniscient self, sending me a message to prompt me out of the drudge that my life had become.

Ironically, my spirit soul appeared in the dead of the night at a time I was both confused and confounded by the complexities of existence. Never to be dubbed the life of the party, I withered away in silence, aged and frail, and relegated myself to a series of meaningless chores that I called work, when in reality it was nothing short of an escape that I had ingenuously designed for myself.

Trapped in a cage I had constructed, I desperately sought the key to the door. Lost and forlorn I looked deeper and deeper within myself and at times I was convinced that my spirit soul was a result of my own inner exploration that had somehow seen the light, fuelled by my own eagerness and desperation. I think the need, the unspoken desire that lies within all of us, hidden between the crevices of the mind, somehow took wings and in full flight it manifested itself under the shade of darkness to be my eternal companion.

Sometimes I am convinced that we never spoke but in reality I know we did. There are times when my imagination gets the better of me and because my spirit soul appears consistently close to the stroke of midnight there was the possibility that it was an unworldly visitor that had somehow bonded with me and for a brief moment had decided to walk again among the living to give me some respite from my sorrows.

I have heard of such stories before, when the need for companionship is so great that the spirits of past and present congregate. The dead and the living meet in unison and mingle like cherished friends.

That is what my spirit soul was, a cherished friend. It sent me into a frenzy at one stage, when it failed to appear. This was when I reasoned that it may be a lingering spirit of the dead and I searched the local obituaries for a name that did not exist. Then I reasoned maybe it didn't have a name. My spirit soul was intent on taking a person who had been caught up in the mundane routine of life and turn him into something that was wholly different.

The mind, I'm told is a multi faceted instrument that has the ability without the knowledge of the body to trigger certain events. Its incredible incredulity takes the consciousness by storm and the minds of all persons, past and present are linked. It is this infinite bond, this inexplicable linkage, that makes the impossible possible.

As a young man I was fascinated by this dubious state of the mind and in my eagerness to explore its full potential,

I began reading earnestly on the subject. Maybe it was this un-withering taste for knowledge that had somehow, changed the complexion of my existence, by inducing the spirit soul to take an active part in my life.

I am convinced it was karma. I am convinced that my uninspiring state of existence is a result of karma, and that the intervention of the spirit soul was a result of karmic consequences.

All actions have a reaction and all contributions have consequences either positive or negative and all negative actions have retributions. It is the cosmic rule of existence that never falters. I am convinced that it is my karma, the unseen and often unfelt factor that manipulated my life and that had brought the spirit soul into being. I was bonded with the spirit soul for all eternity, not only for this lifetime but for all lifetimes. But I was fortunate, from a young age; I had come under her patronage – the Goddess.

The Goddess is kind, merciful in her way and she protects those that she loves. She mitigates the affects of negative karma. There is no greater instrument of torture than one's own emotions. The pain is unbearable, beyond anything that can be inflicted by physical implements. It is the excruciating pain that one feels inside that can plunge a person into untold misery.

I was part of the material world, this uninspiring existence that confines us to mundane living and I understood this well. I sometimes think that the spirit soul was more than an apparition. Its essence was more spiritual than it was physical and this allowed it to transgress time and space. So it always existed with me, and while I was confined to this physical realm, it wasn't.

I didn't think I was possessed for nothing that's seeks to possess the body of another would seek to do any good but the spirit soul has only sought to guide me in the right direction and therefore I reasoned I was not possessed.

After our initial meeting, like fleeting spirits in the night, a meeting which I am certain took place but am uncertain if I had met another living person, it gradually seeped into my soul and blended into my existence. It became the little voice in my head and the moment I erred it stepped in to steer me in the right direction.

I did make some enquiries, to find out if it really existed. The telephone call seemed so real but even that could have been my deepest desires unfolding into an unexpected conversation. We all need to be loved, I'm told. I decided to retrace my steps from the preceding days before our meeting which I'm convinced took place.

Negative karma travels for thousands of miles like a dark cloud in search of its victim who is related to the body that it was released from. Karma is real and it moves and changes shape, like a shape shifter it takes on different forms and assumes different identities. Good karma comes in the form of celestial beings and angels. Bad karma comes in the form of evil beings whose hearts are murkier than that of the vilest men, who seek to pollute and contaminate everything that they touch.

The spirit soul, I think, was there to guide me in my darkest hour and by doing so it was forever ingrained to my being and that made it a part of my existence. Without it, I would wither away like a flower in the desert.

Karma is a not an intangible factor. To the contrary it is very much alive, as subtle as a midsummer breeze; negative karma stalks its prey, lurking behind the darkest corners. It is an opportunist that never fails to seize the moment and it is only prudent to trust no one in one's darkest hour. No doubt I was destined to go through a bad patch; I could feel the vibes reverberating off the four walls that constantly surrounded me.

I was a captive of my own design, a fugitive of my own making. Solitude to me appeared to be the best avenue. I trusted no one, not even my closest associates. To be in the company of many, during the rough patch I was going through would only make me more vulnerable.

That was what I feared most, my own karma. My own misdeeds that kept haunting me, from a past that I was running from, and it was my deepest desire to pass from the last life to the next unscathed for I feared that I would not be able to fulfill my destiny.

I was destined to die at a young age and three times did the fates try to tear me asunder and three times did I escape but the events that had transpired had sapped me dry and I remained an empty shell devoid of any emotion until the fateful day when the spirit soul made up its mind to intervene. It was an infusion of emotion, the feelings that had long ceased to exist, resurfaced again after the meeting.

Karma is a perfect equation that balances itself out with time. It is a factor that is brought forward from another life, from another place and it had a profound effect on everyone. I am rarely moved by people or emotion and by nature, being the ideal scorpion, I was suspicious of everyone.

Life progressed in this manner for years and I was never able to ascertain for sure if the spirit soul existed for real or otherwise but it existed without doubt in my mind.

As the years progressed the spirit soul found a permanent place in the back of my mind, appearing only at odd intervals, when I had time to think and ponder, which was to say the least, minimal, until one day I made an uninspiring comment to someone and the memories came flooding back.

I decided that my approach required overt discretion. It had to be quiet yet open and I was way past the stage in my life where I was perturbed by any show of emotion.

We met in secret in the labyrinths of my mind, my spirits soul, and I. Here we had wonderful times unperturbed by the rest of the world, sharing our music, in the company of nature and in fine settings. We shared everything with each other and we kept our news to ourselves. We were selfish and we didn't want the world to know. We didn't want anyone to know. If the truth be told we were afraid. We were afraid that is if someone knew, they would try to tear us apart and for many years I ruthlessly guarded this secret.

I was no super sleuth and mind exploration is painstaking work involving hours of prayers and meditation. Mantras help focus ones thoughts and channel them in the appropriate direction. Once the mind achieves the ability to focus it is able to discern truth from fiction, fact from myth.

In my mind I began to explore the many facets of the spirit soul, its personality, its essence, its nature and its character. The spirit soul was the master of my ship but I could mold it to suit my designs.

All things in life had a purpose and no meeting is inconsequential. Our small actions could lead to dire consequences. Inaction is just as potent an instrument as action. Even if we don't do anything wrong, it doesn't mean we have done everything right and eventually it pans out to be the same thing.

Positive emotions require positive actions which sometimes is abstention. It takes more control to restrain than to act and the mental exertion of doing so is beyond most people. People feel compelled to act and the common assumption is that one's emotions are only genuine if one acts. Nothing could be further from the truth. Genuine emotions are not only apparent but manifestly apparent and it is unmistakable in design.

Matrimonial bonds for example, endure for an eternity, forged in flames in our first lifetime, they transcend time and space and continue through to each life unfettered. Sometimes the lines get blurred because of karma and it takes a bit longer or we may never meet the person but that is a result of inappropriate actions.

We can only mitigate karma, we cannot change it. We don't just like someone without reason and the instant attraction or appeal is due to a bond sealed in blood eons ago. The act of marriage attested to by the flames of passion and witnessed by the Gods in heavens cannot be diminished under any circumstances and the bond once sealed cannot be broken. It will endure the test of time. It will last for as long as the sun remains and when that sun is no more the partners will merge and become one.

I realized that this bond that I had with the spirit soul was eternal, spiritual in essence and therefore inexplicably linked to my existence. I tried initially to detach myself, to break away from the bond but it was always there lurking in the corners of my mind and when my body was at its weakest, following the daily departure of the sun and sleep lulled me into false comfort, it would appear in my dreams. At first it showed me places, then it showed me events and finally I could converse with it in normal fashion.

Initially my dreams appeared to be nothing more than random images, that made no sense but eventually I began to realize that these events were indeed true and had happened or were likely to happen and that my spirit soul had given me the gift of clairvoyance. Somehow the spirit soul had triggered this unexplained ability to see into the future and it had managed to help breach the barrier between the living and the dead.

The dead I realized were not unlike the living, and this knowledge that I had acquired after I had met the spirit soul sometimes made me question if I had indeed met a living person, or if it was someone who existed no longer in the world of the living.

The dead have desires and longings just like the living and they sought like the rest of us to convey their messages across to the people they loved and sought more than anything else to be around them. The division between good and evil does not end with death and I realized that we ought to cleanse the soul before anything else because if the soul is tainted than all else is tarnished.

The need to fulfill their cravings makes them reach out to us. It is a delicate matter and not for the faint hearted. I have never been perturbed or even remotely unsettled by the dead. To the contrary they have always filled me with sadness and sorrow, especially when they refuse to cross over because they are bound by the chains of love.

As I understood it, the "crossing over" does not happen or occur instantly at the time of death, and the soul that lingers after the body departs needs to atone for its sins. This period of being in the void, in between the living and the dead makes the process all the more difficult and in some cases the spirit refuses to cross over lingering, for many years if not hundreds.

Not all spirits are bound to the void by love. Others are confined by baser desires and once these desires fester, it drives them, to commit untold sins. Bad karma attracts these unfortunate souls and nothing good transpires in their presence. Karma like the marital bond transcends time and it doggedly follows its victim until such time as their sins have been cleansed. There are two sets of laws in this world, the laws of men and the laws of God and it is prudent to comply with both.

I knew I had transgressed these laws at some instance in my past existence and this violation had cost me dearly. But nothing lasts forever and upon paying the karmic dues the soul is free again to traverse the mortal plane. New souls must be cautions not to reject the laws of the universe.

The universe works on a balance, and when this balance is tilted it creates a ripple effect that may have severe repercussions. Therefore it is only wise to stay on the side of caution.

The spirit soul is pure. Positive karma tries to balance negative karma and in the tussle that follows the mind and body, unless they are physically and spiritually sound, degenerate and both are reduced to a vehicle that is moved by opposing forces. Clarity of thought is crucial but it isn't always possible and the period of confusion that follows the battle between good and bad karma leaves the mind and body dazed.

I existed in this state for many years and the inexplicable effects of negative karma at times overwhelmed or out did any benefit I could have derived from positive actions. Over time however, I began to change and take positive steps to unsettle the effects of negative karma. This was best done by doing good deeds and I found social activism a means of negating the effects of bad karma.

With the help of what I can only perceive to be a spirit that existed within me, I began to slowly plod forward, and erase bit by bit the long lasting consequences of actions done in the past. I pondered on what had caused such a dire aftermath and the answer of course was in the life I had led in the past. The present life is a result of a past life and the sequence that follows sways to a beat that was drummed out decades if not centuries ago.

Upon death the soul doesn't always migrate to a new body. Before the transmigration of the soul can take place, there is a period where the body is confined to a vacuum or an existence of non existence. It is alive but without form or shape normally affixed to a certain location and at other times moving fleetingly with the wind from one location to the other. This is the spirit that lingers after death.

The spirit remains for reasons that are best known only to it and refuses to make the journey from death to the next life or the afterlife and continues to navigate between the world of the living and the world of the dead. In this transcendental state the spirit continues to influence the life of others.

The journey from death to the next life is not without peril and during this journey the spirit must be guided by its living relatives. It can easily lose its way and remain in the void, never failing to return to its favorite haunts if given the slightest opportunity.

It carries with it all the emotional baggage that it has inherited from the life it led and those memories remain fresh in the mind even after death. The spirit finds it difficult to break away from the life it had embraced and in most cases tries to return.

Death is an eventuality that one needs to prepare for. We are constantly reminded that it can occur at anytime, and it can come without a moment's notice but most people fail to prepare for the final journey and our emotional attachments keep us from making the final detachment. The failure to do so keeps us bound to the material world and draws the spirit back like an invisible magnet.

The problems that we face in the present life are due to our actions in the past life and in order for us to overcome the sometimes unexpected obstacles or that unexpected turn of events that occur without prior notice we have to return to our past life.

Nothing happens without notice and all things are a consequence of actions or inactions. Inaction is sometime just as bad as wrong action. We may not have necessarily done the wrong thing but a failure to the right thing in accordance with the laws of karma, is just as bad.

DHAYANAM II

"The mind is an automated diary that records all events, past, present and future and stores it in a vast library that is known as the sub-conscious or the super consciousness" – Sierra Shea, teacher and mentor – Hawks Nest.

I was born with the concept of good and evil ingrained in me and it gave me a simplistic view of all things. I categorized everything in this manner. The year was 1017 NW * more than a thousand years after the demise of the Empire. It had disfranchised and fragmented to smaller sects governed by a religious order that ruled from Hawks Nest.

This was our land, that of our fathers, and that of their fathers before them. It is from here that our armies once rode out, in search of either fame or fortune, true to our faith. We were once an Empire governed by faith, ruled by leaders who were first priests, then warriors, and we styled ourselves warrior priests.

We came from various sects and wore the colors of our sects. Each sect was governed by an appointed leader who was not elected but born. The mantle of leadership in our sphere was a birth right, granted at the time of birth to him or her that the fortunes smiled upon.

For a leader to be born, the astrological configuration had to be just right, and the planets had to be aligned accordingly for a child to be crowned the leader of a sect. The planets gave their consent by ensuring that they were aligned in the appropriate manner. Only in this way can the child, be protected from the evils that hound and harrow the leader of a sect.

I was born into the most powerful sect of the time and my birth was a mystery even to the most austere priest. I was a gift child, unexpected and a welcome surprise to a sect that was leaderless. I remember as a child, a priest, much revered and respected, walked up to me. He looked into my eyes and blessed me with a mantra. As he repeated the words, I could feel its effects reverberate through my soul.

If he had hoped to surprise me with his powers, he was sorely mistaken. I looked into his eyes, and stared right into his soul, and saw his innermost secrets. The man never looked me in the eye again.

Mantras had a profound effect on me and I was content when I heard the lines repeated correctly. It was music to my soul. I liked the language of the Gods. I had an affinity to it and it pleased me endlessly to know that I had an unexplained rapport with it.

I don't know much about my parents but my father was schooled in both the white and black arts, and he was feared and revered. I was born in the favorable position of being able to master both.

I understood at an early age that life was merely a transition, from one existence to another. We exited through one door, upon death and walked down a long corridor to pass through another door to the present life. Along the passage looming large is karma. The soul that walks along the corridor has to contend with karma and has to repent for its sins. For those who had led a righteous life the walk is short, like a stroll in a magical park. For those who had succumbed to the senses the walk was longer, sometimes along a dark, unlighted trail. They stalled and stumbled many times before eventually finding the right door.

For those who had lead a good life, the doors on either side were white, and for those who had lead an ungodly life, the doors on either side were black, sometimes pitch black. This was not my first life nor was it my last, but all my lives were eventful in some way or another.

I was not raised by my parents but by a lady who was always dressed in red, in the gowns of a priest, with flowing jet black hair that never turned white despite the passage of time. I did meet my birth parents once, when I was about eight but it was this lady that raised me. I was told much later, she had brought me back from the brink of death when I was an infant.

The day I was born a ferocious storm raged through the kingdom, swaggering and bullying its way through. At the first light of dawn a black cloud crept over the horizon; it thundered within and the lord of storm unleashed his minnows. Over the hills and over the plains, heralds of the storm inched closer and the Gods of the abyss rose up.

The prince of the underworld broke the dams of the nether world and the God of war threw down the dykes. The judges of hell raised their torches and lit the land with livid flame. The people cried out in despair and their voices shot up to the heavens. The God of storm turned daylight into darkness and he smashed the land like a teacup, with his war hammer.

The tempest and floods raged for a whole day gathering fury as the day progressed, raging together like warring factions. It poured over the people like the tide of battle. The holy man could not see his brother and the Gods could not see the people. At dawn of the following day the storm subsided and the air was still.

Farms were laid to waste by the deluge. Water swarmed through the neatly tilled land and did not subside until days later. By the time the sun came out the ground had turned to mud and sludge. Many died from the initial down pour and many others died later from hunger and starvation. The population was reduced by one third. After that, no calamity befell the land in the time that I was there.

Prayers and religious rites were routine for us all. We did it from sunrise to sunset in between our studies, in addition to fine tuning our prowess with our weapons. We dressed moderately in cotton garments dyed in yellow, our shirts loose and our pants baggy. No one could mistake us for gentry despite our mannerly conduct but they feared us more than any gentry or king.

It was not that we ruled with an iron fist, we had no intention of doing so, it was just that we were skilled practitioners of the arts both the white and the black arts and we practiced our skills with vigor. Those that lived within the precincts of the stone temple decorated their altars with incense and sweet smelling flowers while others who lived as hermits decorated their altars with good deeds and then there were those who confined themselves to burial grounds, who decorated their altars with skulls and bones. We were all blessed with a gift we called the talent that separated from the rest of the world. Those who had graduated were free to use their "talent" to reach out to the Gods of Heaven or the Gods of Hell.

Only those that were exceptionally gifted were admitted to Hawks Nest. There they lived; their lives shrouded in secrecy under a veil of religious rectitude. In most cases their existence was erased from all records. Once they had passed through the ironclad gates of the sanctuary they existed only in name. Some who had achieved greatness made their way into the folds of legends and folklore.

In prayer, we called upon Zonu, the lord of the heavens, he who has stood glorious in deeds and he who has been celebrated from the dawn of humanity. We called upon him to cherish us in his keep, to nourish us with his blessings, to shower us with his love and to cover us with his glory.

We called upon the mighty bird of prey, Eyry, the unfaltering hawk, to protect us from all evil while we performed our prayers. We called upon the teacher of the Gods, Helbig, to guide us and to preserve the knowledge that we had acquired while performing the rites.

We worshiped the three syllable word. The word that was the sound of nothing and the sound of all things; it was the sound of the beginning and the sound of the end. It was the sound of the past, the present and the future.

When we venerate the word, we venerate the Brahmatma, the super soul that resides in the fourth dimension. By adulating the Brahmatma we also deified our own soul which is part of the collective super soul.

We were all one in the beginning, at one with the super soul and at one with the cosmos but our mind is dual faceted by nature and the conscious mind, that controls the senses became too absorbed with fulfilling sensory needs and thus we drifted farther and farther away from the super soul until the soul that was in the beginning the size of a full grown man shrank to become nothing more than a tiny light that sometimes flickered depending on the nature of the conscious mind.

The duplicity of existence therefore is a result of the conscious mind. In order to realize our full potential we have to realize the Brahmatma or the super soul.

The sects didn't worship like normal. They in reality were in touch with the Gods and Goddesses more than anyone else. Their worship was sometimes ritualistic in essence and at other times not. They offered themselves and hence there was no need for any other offering. It was the ultimate sacrifice and the sects demanded it. Our loyalty belonged to our chosen Gods or Goddesses.

The leaders of the sects are bonded to their Gods or Goddesses and they continue to exist for the duration of time. While the normal man seeks liberation from the cycle of birth and death, leaders of the sect are born over and over again and at each birth they move closer to the ultimate reality.

To them is granted the most unique of mantras and this they guard with their lives, because their existence depends on the mantras. I would learn much later that no leader of a sect rises to the position with clean hands. Their hands more often than not are bloodied in ways none could perceive.

Having realized the Brahmatma, it was then time to give the Brahmatma shape and form, and in our sect the living Goddess was the incarnate of the Brahmatma and we worshipped her in the form that she was.

The territories, the remains of the former Empire, were divided between the sects and like kings to a kingdom the rulers of the sects ruled with absolute authority. I understood early in life that it was my destiny to rule and that it was granted to me at birth.

All the sects were governed by a supreme leader, who resided in Hawks Nest. He was a true monastic, and rarely left the shelter of the sanctuary. It was the most guarded sanctuary on the planet and none ventured to Hawks Nest without an invitation. To do so would mean certain death.

It stood high in the mountains, a large walled fortification built on a rugged land that covered a vast area. The leader of all sects lived within its walls guarded by the most lethal warriors. When Hawks Nest roared the world trembled. I as would be leader of the most powerful sect had my seat reserved for me, beside the chosen overlord in the throne room.

I grew up in isolation and seclusion and rarely got to play with other children. I didn't miss it. I'd rather spend the hot humid afternoons that were peculiar to the south, indoors surrounded by books. I was a veracious reader who had an enormous appetite for knowledge and I would read without fail. The word for knowledge in language of the Gods was also the word for growth which meant to say we grew with knowledge.

After my sixteenth birthday we moved to the north and I found the climate more accommodating. I liked the cold more than I liked the heat and many years' later people would say that I had icy waters running in my veins but that mattered little to me. I knew the objective was more important than the general perception.

That was a good year for me. I got to see the world a bit more. My guardian and I with a handful of escorts traversed the northern half of an Empire that had by now almost turned to dust.

The route that we had chosen eventually took us to the foot of the Gorgon Mountains where we stumbled on a campsite inhabited by hunter gatherers with instincts as sharp as their swords. The "white witch" my guardian whispered in my ear and I bowed my head instantly in obsequious but remained silent, quite certain that matters would come to light in time. My guardian had the uncanny habit of dropping hints and giving me advance warnings of events that were about to transpire.

We rode towards a large tent made of animal hide. Little children were running around clad in clothes made of animal skin; their legs were adorned with furry boots. I smiled. As we rode up the flap of the tent flew open and a tall slim lady, her skin as pale as the snow that covered the ground, her eyes the color of brown emeralds walked out and kneeled, head bowed, in front of us. It was a mark of respect to the living Goddess, and my guardian made a sign, signaling her to lift her head. She liked the witch; I could tell and if the truth be told, so did I. She was enchantingly pretty. "Greetings Goddess" said the witch and pointed to a young girl that had followed closely behind unnoticed.

I couldn't help but stare at the girl. She looked almost identical to the witch, a miniature duplicate that was nearly my age, food stains clearly visible on her brown tunic. Her hair disheveled, she looked like she had just risen out of bed. She made her way forward, towards us, her footsteps leaving small imprints on the snow.

I turned my head and looked at my guardian. I was seated on a brown mare beside her. She read my thoughts as she often did and said to me "she's you". I was confused, "so now there are two of us?" I asked. My guardian gave me a playful nudge. I chuckled. I instantly liked my other half; she represented a disorderliness that I found refreshing.

My other half looked rather distracted and couldn't stop staring at us, "child" I thought to myself with a gentle toss of the head. "Young witch" chided my guardian.

"She is very pretty, like you, white witch" said my guardian. The white witch smiled. She blushed and her cheeks turned red. She looked all the prettier. We got off the horses, the coat of the brown mare which I rode, uncannily resembled the brown tunic that the girl had on her. Only hers had morsels of food attached to it.

I walked up to the young girl. We became instant friends, and ran off to play in the snow. We got tired after a bit and soon decided to sit down and watch the sun spiral upwards to its zenith. We never said much. It was like we knew what the other was thinking and right now we wanted to sit down and watch the sun, and lose ourselves in thought. My guardian was right, she was like me a thinker who no doubt spent hours pondering on things that often seemed irrelevant at that time but had a strange way of cropping up in the future. Maybe it was a type of clairvoyance that we were both gifted with. She too was gifted with the talent and it was as strong with her as it was with me.

As the day brightened up men and women could be seen around the camp. The men were rarely on horseback and the women went about their business on foot, making their way around the encampment busing themselves with their chores. A few of them stopped to smile but most of them ignored us. The scent of cooking meat soon filled the air, and we were both hungry. I was wondering when it would be time for lunch when I heard my guardian calling out to me. I stood up and my little friend did the same. I took her hand in mine; something compelled me to do so, and led the way back to the witch's tent.

I pushed the flap open and my little friend ran in. "What's you name" I asked her, a bit later …. Better late than never, I thought. "Chandika" she replied. "You can call me Chandi". It was a beautiful name. The white witch interrupted, in a soothing tone "you are bonded together forever, you know" she said. Well I didn't mind, two of me must be better than one, and I liked my new friend. There was something about her; I felt it when I touched her hand, it seeped instantly into my soul, and I felt her spirit gradually flow through my veins.

I had a quick look around the tent; it was filled with idols, trinkets, figurines, and an assortment of charms and potions in small jars and beakers in a range of colors. It was prettily arranged and I could tell the witch was extremely conscious about cleanliness which was the correct path to religious enlightenment. I approved. My friend gave me a little nudge with her shoulder and whispered in my ear "You're getting a bit ahead of yourself aren't you" I giggled and she did the same. She could read my thoughts.

"Come children" the witch called out. We obeyed and sat down on a thick blanket. She handed me stew made from buffalo meat, potatoes and wild onions. I lifted a spoonful to my mouth and guzzled it down almost instantly. The witch was an amazing cook, and her food tasted delicious.

Before we left I was made to take my new friend's hand and the witch tied a little flower knot that bonded the both of us together. We were made to kneel in front of her and she blessed us both. As we were about to walk out of the tent I kissed my little friend on the cheek and she blushed instantly a pink glow appearing on her face. I knew then that we would never be apart and that we would always be together for all eternity.

Over the year, we visited the white witch's camp regularly and in that time I got to know my friend well. We had wonderful times together and that was most probably the best year of my life. I travelled around with my guardian and learnt as much as I could

My seventh year was the pivotal year for me. It was the year I was taken to Hawks Nest, to be initiated in the order and become the leader of the most powerful sect in the land.

On the first day of the year I stood outside the small temple behind a concrete building that was our meager living quarters, in a distant land, far up in the north and looked over the horizon. A cold chilly wind blew from the north biting into me and for a brief second I almost buckled in the cold. "War" she said. I trembled, not from the cold but by the icy undertones in her voice. "Are you all right?" a little voice flashed in my head, my little friend had felt it too. "I'm fine" I replied.

According to rumors, which we confirmed later, Dashia was under siege. The kingdom was located along the banks of the Darya River; its capital Dashra had been taken. It was an ailing kingdom that was on the verge of collapse. Once an important trade route that linked the east to the west, it had declined over time, but remained an important artistic and religious stronghold. It was a bitter loss that sent ripples that were felt by all leaders in the religious echelon.

It was not a migration but a planned movement of people. It was not overrun by those fleeing from war either.

The sects were sworn to protect all who sought refuge, regardless of who they were. This was an attack, cold, unmitigated and planned. I was summoned to Hawks Nest.

It was a perilous journey, to a fortress located high up in the Forbidden Mountains. It was surrounded by sharp jagged rocks, unassailable by normal means and the path that led to its iron clad gates was steep and narrow. We set out on a cold winter morning the second day of the year, my guardian and I, in the company of pack horses that carried our food and other provisions, from a remote village, secluded in the eastern border of Saurland, a small impoverished agricultural state and headed westwards to Hawks Nest.

I had a thick fur coat on while my guardian remained in her red cotton garments unperturbed by the weather. She was never moved by the changing vicissitudes of climatic conditions and was ever stolid in all situations. She was pale; her skin, like that of the white witch, as pure as un-melted snow. She was no taller that five six, but she was as sturdy as an oak and as slim as willow. Her eyes always sparkled like dazzling blue sapphires. Her jet black hair was tied neatly behind in a knot and despite the passage of time, she never aged.

The journey was quiet with the occasional snow storm, when we had to shelter in the thatched homes of villagers, who were more than kind to us. In return we generously shared our food with them. Most of them were farmers and the torrid weather meant that they could grow little crops. They survived on what they had managed to salvage from the summer. The land was fertile when the sun was out but even in the abundantly rich soil nothing would grow in winter.

We moved from village to village as we plodded our way to Hawks Nest. The journey was not always drab and the sun did shine occasionally which made for a lovely day. The trees were naked and I had a grand time breaking off the branches to light fires. I was never certain if it was my skill at picking suitable branches or if it was my guardians magic that set the twigs ablaze. I was not the best of campers and as the years dragged on, I would manage my armies with the barest minimum. Time I felt was better utilized proactively.

By the time we reached Hawks Nest, the moon had completed two cycles. A guide was waiting for us at the foot of the Forbidden Mountain, he was dressed in the yellow robes of a monk, like me, not uncommon in these parts, and from below, when we looked up we could see that the entire upper half of the mountain was covered with structures of different sizes. Some were monasteries, some were built for housing purposes and others were built to defend the insurmountable fortress.

We had passed many monasteries on our way to Hawks Nest, small and quaint, housing no more than a few monks. These were more monastic communities and prayers were a daily routine, some prayed in their homes and others visited temples with offerings of fruits and flowers.

Governance was by monastic law and the sects were never hesitant to mete out punishment when the situation required it. It kept the communities operating in orderly fashion. The monasteries also served as a warehouse where excess food was stored and this was important during difficult times that were sometimes brought about by unexpected changes in weather conditions or new additions to the families or the communities. It was an equation to not only balance the food supplies but also to cater for any eventualities that might arise.

The monastic citadels were located beneath the watchful eye of Hawks Nest and that made the monks exceptionally cautious. There have been instances of corrupt monks hoarding food in the past but the criminals once uncovered were brought to swift and often painful justice.

Our guide was lean and tall, his skinned was unusually tanned, and from all appearances he didn't look native to these parts. He had a bow and a quiver of arrows strapped to his back. A sheathed sword hung loosely by his side, his hands no doubt could move at the rate of knots to reach for the hilt should the situation require it.

*NW is an abbreviation for "New World". It is used in reference to dates on the modern calendar. The modern calendar starts on the day after the collapse of the Grand Empire.

DHAYANAM III

"And he approached the angel of death and begged and pleaded for his aid. Finally the keeper of the abyss relented, and unlocked the door to the deep dark dungeon, where the fallen and demons were bound in chains" – Chronicles of Serpentine.

Our guide was almost six feet tall and the color of his eyes matched that of his hair, black with a lustrous shine, eyes of steel that never looked to miss a beat. "Welcome" he said, lifting his right hand, palm outward, in customary fashion, the sign of universal acceptance.

My guardian acknowledged his greeting with a tilt of her head. I flashed him a meek smile, too tired to do anything else, my limbs were sore and my muscles ached from continuous riding.

He was sitting astride a black stallion, its eyes the color of flaming rubies. I was intrigued. I was tempted to take a closer look. "How did it get those eyes?" I asked. The man smiled. "Not now little one, I'll explain later" my guardian intervened. He introduced himself. "My name is Bozak" he said.

"I'll be your guide" he continued and turned his horse towards a steep cliff. "What is the latest news?" my guardian inquired. "Listen" a voice said inside my head. It was Chandi speaking to me, I smiled. It was always a pleasure listening to her voice. I felt drowsy but I stayed awake because I knew what was about to be said was important.

"The armies that invaded Dashia are moving towards Lamunia. If Lamunia falls, they will move towards Amestria and if it falls they will be at our doorstep". My guardian remained silent, listening to the warrior.

Amestria was a sacred kingdom that was located southwest of Lamunia. It was the home of the alchemic sisterhood. According to the ancient scrolls the High Priestess Tiara descended from the heavens and shared her knowledge with the sisterhood. The wisdom of Tiara was condensed in a series of green crystalline tablets that became known as the sacred tablets of Tiara.

The tablets contain in whole the science of alchemy. Alchemy is the combination of matter and spirit, a unification of Tiara (matter) and her consort Maat (spirit). The teachings were initially kept secret available only to selected members of the sisterhood.

"Is it to be the end?" asked Bozak. My guardian shook her head, "Not the end but a new beginning" she said. We both looked puzzled. She lowered her head and kissed me. "I fear for you my son", "I fear for what is to become of the both of you" she said.

I was taken aback by what I heard. I wasn't certain why she feared for Chandi or me but her warning sounded ominous. We both had her and the white witch to protect us, so I wasn't too perturbed or disturbed by what I had heard but Chandi, the other half remained attentive. She'd fill me in later if I missed something. I dozed off. When I woke up again it was nightfall and it was almost time to make camp. Bozak and my guardian were still talking.

"It will take them years to defeat Lamunia but eventually it will fall, won't it?" asked Bozak. My guardian nodded her head, "and eventually they will take Amestria too" he continued. "Possibly" said my guardian.

"The Brahmatma the supreme soul has decreed thus but from him I have obtained eternal protection for my children, who do but his bidding" she continued. "And the rest?" asked Bozak. "They will be forgiven once they have repented sufficiently". Bozak nodded. "Those who have mastered the art of killing without attracting karmic reprisals however will escape its consequences" she added.

We came across a small mountain creek, and we got off our horses to set up camp for the night. My guardian readied a meal; while I drifted in and out of sleep. Even the aromatic scent of sweet meats prepared with a blend of exotic spices couldn't prevent my eyelids from closing.

It was a long journey to the citadel and the climb lasted for days. In that time we passed many small structures, living quarters that housed the residents of Hawks Nest. The dwellings were located on either side of a narrow path that lead to the summit of the Forbidden Mountain, built on small plots of flat land that were bordered by steep cliffs.

They looked like they could fall off at anytime. If a natural calamity were to strike it would be nothing short of disastrous. They were precariously situated but despite their dubious setting these structures had managed to withstand the test of time. I couldn't help but wonder if there was some unseen magic that held it all together.

We arrived at the ironclad gates of Hawks Nest just after midmorning; Bozak led the way while my guardian and I followed. The packhorses were located at the rear. We had made it just in the knack of time. Our supplies were almost depleted; we had shared most of our food with the villagers that we met along the way.

As we pulled up, I could hear the sound of loud trumpets blaring away and I became instantly alert. A fitting welcome for a leader, I thought to myself. "Don't get too ahead of yourself" a sharp voice rang inside my head. I smiled.

The gates swung open and we went through. As we rode past the main citadel I noticed that there were armed guards to the right and the left, clad not in the loss fitting robes of a monk, but in armor made of black steel and leather, their swords sheathed menacingly at their sides. They were lean like Bozak and looked liked they had been repeatedly put to the test. Battle hardened veterans; all of them, and they looked every inch the part.

I looked into their eyes and I was instantly reminded of the stallion, wild, untamable, and incessantly loyal. Before I could speak my guardian uttered a single word "Chandi". I smiled; my little friend was more influential than I thought. It made sense, these were warriors and they worshipped a warrior Goddess, to the extent that she became a part of all of them. I bowed my head and uttered a simple prayer to the warrior Goddess, my other half, Chandi.

The parade of soldiers lined up from the iron gates to the flight of steps that lead up to the main citadel. They stood in full attention on both sides and I was elated. Maybe it was my ego getting the better of me.

All around us I could see other buildings, living quarters mostly, with the odd monastery or chapel located in between. It did not look like a planned arrangement that had been drawn up by a skilled builder. The shapes and structures were not in unison and looked like they were erected as and when the need arose. When we reached the foot of the steps, Bozak got off his horse, and we did the same, leaving their care to the guards who stood ready to take their reins. We followed the warrior through the doorway into a lavishly decorated throne room.

The walls and the floors were lined with thick red carpets, the color of a Mogok Ruby, and on either side there were neatly arranged seats hundreds of them. It was by no means a small room and the roof was hand painted, depicting scenes of battles long gone, when the Empire was almost at the brink of exhaustion with defeat staring it in the eye, relentlessly pursued by ruthless foes. One by one the soldiers perished, limb and sinew extricated from their bodies and their bones ground to dust.

According to the legend, the gates of the abyss had been opened and from its depths thick smog rose to the sky that eventually blotted out the sun. The earth was covered in darkness and the angel of death led his army of demons that took the shape of locusts with stings of scorpions. The armies of the abyss tortured men for seven days and seven nights and on the eight day when the sun returned, the Empire had crumbled.

I looked ahead and I saw two seats, evenly placed beside each other. The seat on the right was vacant but the seat on the left was occupied by a bald man, lean, almost thin. His body looked like it had been starved. He was almost six feet tall. He looked old and worn out, and I could tell that the years had taken their toll on him. I tried to ascertain his age from his appearance but there was no correlation. From all accounts he was hundreds of years old.

He stood up when he saw me and bowed his head humbly his hands clasped together, a sign of marked respect that was directed at my guardian. She smiled. No one knew his name; it was never to be mentioned under any circumstances. His existence was always shrouded in secrecy, hidden by occult. His duties were to direct the sects and my duties, as I would later learn was to enforce his directives.

We walked up to him and as we drew closer I could make out the creases on his face that resembled the cracks of an old leather bound volume, the telltale signs of wear and tear were, abundantly apparent. He looked frail but beneath his feeble exterior I could sense steel, cold and unadulterated.

Years of being at the helm had gnawed away at him leaving behind an anorexic frame. As we were about to reach him, my guardian whispered in my ear, "kneel", she said and I quickly obeyed, getting down on one knee. The overlord nodded his head in smiling approval. He raised his right hand, palm outward, before pointing to the seat on the right, signaling for me to rise and take my seat beside him.

I did so without a second thought, forgetting even my guardian for a moment. It was like the seat was calling out to me and as I sat down; I could feel a surge of power rise within me. It was exhilarating unlike anything I had ever felt before.

I looked at my guardian before I looked at the overlord. She looked as calm as ever, they both did. "Ksamata" he said. The word stood for power, capability, capacity and ability, in the language of the Gods. "All in one" he continued. My heartbeat went up a notch. A voice inside my head called out to me "calm down" it said and instantly I felt the surge that had taken me by surprise dissipate.

I was normal again. "You must learn how to control it, young one", the overlord said. My guardian remained silent looking Godlier than ever, her eyes fixed on me with a hint of steel.

I eased back, and sank deeper into the chair and slumped back. "Arrogance", "it is very presumptuous of you" said the overlord. I remained silent. He smiled. "No matter little one, it's time for your formal induction anyway". "Tomorrow when the omens are just right, and when the planetary alignments are perfect, you will assume your rightful office". I was thrilled; I felt the surge of power within me again. My other half was restless; I could feel her tossing and turning.

We spent the night in the main citadel, our rooms were more than comfortable, mine especially so because it was filled with scrolls and scripts. "You wrote them, you know" said my guardian. I looked surprised, "you wrote them the last time you were here". It must have been in my last birth, she nodded reading my thoughts again. "You were the same then as you are now", she said. "You have known me that long?" I asked. I have always known you she said, since the first day you set foot on this earth. I brought you here. I remained silent.

"You have a partner you know", she said. Now that sounded promising, a new face in the picture. My other half giggled. "I paired you together in your first birth". "What is she liked" I asked, curiosity getting the better of me. "You'll find out soon enough" she replied. That sounded even more promising, I thought. My other half burst into laughter.

I lay in bed that night, eyes wide open, thinking about her, this girl that was my partner. I couldn't help but wonder what she was like. Chandi didn't make matters any better, she kept interrupting, needling me, and I fell asleep laughing at her antics.

I woke the next morning well before sunrise; my guardian had silently walked in and she gently tapped on my shoulder to wake me up. I opened my eyes and instantly remembered that it was the day of my induction. The grogginess disappeared within seconds. I jumped out of bed and quickly got into my robes. I wondered if I should have a bath when my guardian spoke "no need, you have to be as you are" she said. She was like my other half; she could read my thoughts as soon as they popped into my head. I wondered if I had any privacy at all "you do" she said. I gave up.

Lamunia1034:- Triloka stood on top of the parapet that overlooked the vast, vacant space, and stared at the barren rock filled area that lay sprawling in front of the towers, his eyes keenly looking for telltale signs of what was without doubt, an imminent invasion. The fall of Dashia had sent shivers down the spine of its neighboring kingdoms. It had succumbed with relative ease and the next on the list was either Lamunia or Amestria.

**

A young boy slowly walked up a narrow stairway leading to a bell tower, in Amestria. Dressed in the flowing yellow robes of a monk, his thoughts revolved around the routine he had faithfully observed for the last two years. Orphaned at birth, the monastery took him in and he had spent his whole life within its four walls. Each morning he made his way up to the bell tower and there he tugged on a string that sent the chimes of the brass bell reverberating through the small town he lived in.

The boy tugged on the rope at the first sight of sunlight but unlike most days something was different today. The sun appeared without fail and the bell rang promptly but there was something out of the ordinary in the air. The smell of blood and grime drifted in with the morning breeze and a sudden realization struck the boy. War, somewhere out there was a village and its entire population had been laid to waste.

Amestria had been the nucleus of an ancient civilization for almost a thousand years. The essence of a religious culture and the later sectarian influences maintained a vice like grip on its citizens, many of whom were artisans of renowned stature.

That was about to change. Usan, that was the boy's name, was gifted more than most boys his age but his "talent" was kept hidden within the four walls of the monastery that was now his home. The boy repeated a mantra invoking the protection of the fiery God of Nine Treasures who was the guardian of all monastic sanctuaries.

Triloka, kept his ears peeled for the sound of hoofs beating against the harden dirt. It hadn't rained much during the year and the brazen summer heat coupled with the harsh frost of winter had desensitized the land. The crops had withered more than normal and the harvest had been mediocre. Despite the poor yields there was still plenty of food to go around. The stores were overflowing with grain and famine was kept at bay.

The invaders were organized, slow, skilled and meticulous in their approach. They captured one village at a time and a majority of the villages were unprotected. The aggressors stationed themselves well with an army at their back. It was a twofold attack one towards Lamunia and the other into Amestria. If successful the invasion could bring about the ultimate demise of the sects.

Hawks Nest had thus far refused to retaliate. The overlord remained silent and brooded over the attacks. The kingdoms were in a state of confusion. The local militia skilled as it was faced an enemy equally as skilled, adept horsemen who fought well on horseback. They looked liked they had been trained from birth, a peculiar trait of the tribes that inhabited the plains north and west of Dashia.

Weeks went by and Triloka decided he had to witness the strength of the enemy for himself. He rode out in the company of twenty well armed men who disguised themselves as tradesmen. They moved in the dead of the night casually making their way towards Dashra, the capital. There was no rush; the enemy had decided to chip away at them, like a sculptor chipped away at a gravel block, measuring each blow of his hammer to shape the features he desired. Victory would eventually be achieved in an unconventional manner.

It made sense, laying siege to a walled city, was the worst option available and it was only done when there were no other options left. To build large protective shields, armored wagons, and make ready the necessary arms and weapons would take months.

If the general cannot control his emotions and ordered his troops to the swarm the walls, one third of his army would be decimated. This was the type of calamity that could befall an army when attacking a walled city.

Without doubt the enemy was skilled. They hoped to take them without protracted warfare and by doing so they kept their gains intact. To take a walled city, the enemy must have a force of at least ten times that of the city that he hoped to assail and even then if he mistimed his attack, he would lose almost half his troops.

Triloka like a wise general decided to attack the enemies plans. He had plenty of time to think while he was riding. He planned to divide his troops into small contingents, to harass and harrow the enemy as much as possible, to slowdown what was a foreseeable plan to capture the villages and cut off food and other supplies to the kingdom. The plan might take years to succeed and cause great hardship but if unaddressed it would succeed. It had its merits.

He had to access his strengths and men for men on horseback his troops would be beaten. The enemy had superior riding skills. Instead, neatly laid ambushes would suit his purpose more. Instead of attacking the enemy it was better to focus on attacking the enemy's supplies and reinforcements. It would force the enemy to either attack or retreat; an unplanned attack was just as bad as a retreat, he might succeed. Under both circumstances the enemy would suffer severe casualties. Victory to his opponents he decided would come at a high cost. He had to thin the enemies armies where possible.

Prisoners were a problem, they had to be fed and housed and he could never be sure of their loyalty. Given a choice, most of them if freed would go back to the services of their former liege. All the options of taking prisoners alive proved too costly. Hence it was best to deliver a lethal stroke where possible.

They rode into Dashra within days and scouted around for signs of the enemy. They were visible everywhere, in plain sight, men clad in chain mail armed with swords and shields, the winged serpent clearly visible on their breastplates. The serpent was the emissary of the queen of the abyss, sacred to her. According to the myth, it had spirited her away from the Sky God when she was an infant and anointed her queen of the abyss and all things below.

He feared that the gates of the abyss had been opened again and that the demons of the abyss were walking among them. But he had no possible means of ascertaining the truth and there was no rational way a general could base his defense on what sounded like an unfounded hypothesis.

There was nothing unusual about the city with the exception of the lack of imperial guards who no doubt had perished valiantly, he hoped, in defense of Dashra. Unlike other contemporary cities, there weren't many taverns in the city center and the living accommodations for visitors were modest at best.

Triloka and his men checked in to various modest accommodations around the city and subtly inspected the damage that had been done. The assault didn't appear to have left a lasting impact and Dashra didn't look like it had put up too much of a fight. There was no permanent damage and most of its ancient citadels remained intact. It was a gradual takeover that had occurred over time without making too much of an impression. The signs of a weakening monarchy had no doubt induced the attack. Tactically it was a sound ploy and Dashra was taken with its gains intact.

They spent a couple of days within the city premises before leaving. Once they were a good distance away from the city they turned their horses towards the dense forests and rode deeper hinterland. They camped close to the banks of a river and from there, Triloka sent riders out with his orders.

In the weeks that followed small groups of armed men started appearing all over Dashia. They resembled a light cavalry that carried minimal supplies and covered vast areas in a matter of days. They made lethal, clinical strikes, and the invaders were taken by surprised. The winged serpents (as the locals called them) were often cornered and trapped in neatly laid ambushes and pelted to the ground by repeated showers of arrows. In Lamunia and Amestria there was a sudden surge in demand for archers.

The arrowheads were smeared with a rare poison that was concocted by potent magicians. The slightest break in the skin caused by the offending arrow would not heal and over time it would fester and eventually the weakened body would succumb. In this way they hoped to thin the enemy down.

Weeks later news began filtering through Dashia. Groups of armed men had appeared mysteriously and were rummaging the countryside, ruthlessly cutting down anyone who wore the emblem of the winged serpent. They came from nowhere and disappeared as soon as they had struck, leaving behind few witnesses who never survived for long.

Anyone who survived the initial attack died soon after from a mysterious illness that seemed to eat away at them from the inside. The soldiers of Serpentine were caught off guard but they were resourceful and did not hesitate to send in reinforcements. The attack on Lamunia and Amestria was imminent and it was impossible to predict if Triloka's men could stem the tide. The numbers were not in favor of them and Hawks Nest continued to remain silent.

**

It was time. My guardian escorted me out of my room. Bozak was waiting for me outside in the company of guards, who had discarded their armor for the robes of a monk. There were five in total; in yellow turmeric colored robes similar to the one I had on. I of course was delighted. To be crowned head of a sect at the tender age of seventeen was quite an achievement. In all fairness I had inherited the title and it was not something that I had earned, not as yet anyway, but I was certain that there would be plenty of time for that.

It was a long march, first through the passages that connected the rooms to the rear of the citadel into a large backyard in the middle of which was a mountain pond filled with fresh crystal clear blue water. The sun was slowly rising in the east and I could feel its rays touched my skin as it skimmed off the surface of the water. I was asked to strip and made to jump into the pool.

The water was cool and despite the altitude the temperature remained modest. The golden rays of the sun glistened off the drops of water on my skin and I felt the muscles in my body rejuvenate. It was a unique feeling, there was something in the water, maybe it was a fountain of youth like the legend said, I could not be certain, but I was sure they wouldn't want me to get any younger, not at that age.

As I dipped my head in and out of the water monks gathered around the pool and chanted mantras in unison. As soon as they completed one mantra they dipped into a satchel that they had strung across their shoulder and took out petals of flowers that they gently flung into the pool.

DHAYANAM IV

"He was perfect in wisdom, flawless without mention and utterly righteous. Then he grew proud and deviously connived with one third of the angels to usurp the will of the super soul. The angels retaliated and he was cast out into a dark pit that was the abyss" – The keeper of the abyss.

Soon the surface of the water was filled with flower petals. As the sun rose higher the water got warmer, and I felt like I was in a natural heated pool. An hour or so later my guardian motioned for me to step out of the pool. Naked I stepped out dripping with water from head to toe. I was then made to cover my body in turmeric before I was asked to step back into the pool. After that, I was made to repeat the exercise with red powder. The monks continued chanting the whole time.

After the third hour, the monks brought out a makeshift pyre, filled with sandalwood and drops of pure ghee. They lit the fire and continued to chant mantras. A small group of monks gathered around the fire and started chanting the verses, summoning to start with Safa, the God of fire and the righteous messenger of the Gods, the first and foremost of the elements.

Then they called upon the mighty thunderer, the guardian of the heavens "O salutations to Lord Zonu, how fortunate we are to hear with our ears the blessed words of praise, benediction and devotion, in reverence to the lord of the heavens that brings good fortune to all who hear it"

"May we see with our eyes the offerings made to him who is stolid and steadfast in his task, he who is of the race of excellence, he who is greater than any being possessing a soul or a spirit and he who is infinitive in his life and in his grace"

"Exalted from the beginning of time is Zonu, he who has stood glorious in deeds and he who has been celebrated from the dawn of humanity. May he cherish us in his keep, nourish us with his blessings, shower us with his love and cover us with his glory".

"Blessings unto him and unto us; we call upon the mighty Hawk, Eryr to protect us from all evil while we perform our prayers. We call upon Helbig, teacher of the Gods, to guide us and to preserve the knowledge that we acquire during our prayers. Peace to all".

"O praise to the three syllable word, the primordial sound, the eternal sound, the sound of creation, the sound of the universe, the sound of all things and the sound of nothing, the sound of the past, the present and the future, the sound that is indestructible and that is inexhaustible, the sound of the beginning and the end. We ask that our sins be washed away, that our bodies be purified, and that we attain the knowledge that we so honestly and earnestly desire".

An age old passage from the Book of Deeds; it was one of the first passages I was taught. As they continued to chant my mind drifted to the passages from the sacred text. There are four dimensions, the dimension of lines, the dimension of shapes, the dimension of lines, shapes and colors and the dimension of the Brahmatma, the super soul, he who is the be all and end all of all things.

All souls are connected to the super soul and this connection between souls gives all beings a super consciousness through which they can realize the noblest truths. The super consciousnesses or collective consciousness stores the memories of all beings past, present and future. Time is a fixed line with a start and an end and by having access to the super consciousness we can travel the time line. This is best achieved when the body is in a semi conscious or an unconscious state.

In this state the functions of the conscious mind are reduced considerably, and the semi conscious mind or the sub conscious mind gains greater control of the soul. The semi conscious mind is directly linked to the Brahmatma and when this connection is alive we share the consciousness of the super soul.

By the time I stepped out of the pool it was mid afternoon. The sun was right above my head tainted only by the black silhouette of a hawk flying above. Eryr, the might bird had come to bless the proceedings. Hawks Nest was named after the great bird of prey that was the personification of goodness and the arch nemesis of all serpents. So it came as no surprise when I learned much later that our enemies wore the emblem of the winged serpent on their breastplates. An enmity of old had transcended time, I concluded.

The prayers were finished by mid afternoon. As we walked the monks began to disperse, and we were joined by the overlord. I liked the man who carried himself with an air of invisibility when he walked. "How do you feel" he asked. "Much refreshed, most venerated one" I replied. He smiled. "You're learning fast" he said. "Courteous replies will get you everywhere".

My induction was followed by my coronation but sadly that did not include a crown. I was given a set of yellow robes, slightly darker than those that I normally used, the color of ground turmeric and a set of weapons. There was more work than play, many times more, and there was little fun, in the real sense of the word in the company of monks and soldiers.

Hawks Nest became my permanent home, for now anyway. Throughout the year we continued to receive reports of the events that transpired, in Dashia, Lamunia and Amestria. According to the reports that we received some of the troops had deserted the army and rallied under a renegade general. They were launching a counter offensive.

"You have to meet him" said the overload during supper that evening. I was busy dipping my bread in thick broth and stopped momentarily to hear him speak. "You will go alone with, Bozak" said my guardian, her voice firmer than normal but with a hint of playfulness. "You will take your sword, and dress like a normal monk. Take as much supplies as you need" she continued. Bozak who always joined us during meals nodded his head in acknowledgement.

We set out a week later, I was given a brown mare, slightly taller and leaner than most and Bozak sat astride his fiery red eyed black stallion. We took four pack horses with us laden with supplies and if we needed more, we decided that we'd picked them up on the way. I made sure the supplies were packed with lots of dried, salted meat, which I must admit I liked very much. I even packed some in the satchel that I had slung over my shoulder, so I could snack on the way.

Maybe I would get a chance to use my sword in battle. Well maybe not, I decided, after giving it a moment's thought. I was confident enough with my ability but being seventeen I hesitated to take on battle weary opponents. I was progressing well under Bozak's guidance; he was a good teacher with years of experience on the battlefield. The type of blade that we used was from the north and unlike the curved sabers that were more popular in these parts, it had a flat blade, sharpened on both sides that narrowed at the end to a point, attached to the hilt which was protected by a guard at the bottom and decorated with a pommel on top.

It was a perfectly balanced sword forged by the blacksmiths of Hawks Nest. Most swordsmen from the sanctuary had their blade imprinted with mantra or mantras of their choice. I had a simple mantra on mine, in honor to my other half.

Most observers say that I was a better archer than I was a swordsman at that age. I carried a long bow with me in my saddle, equipped with a quiver of arrows. I decided not to lace the arrow heads with poison because I was primarily going to use it for hunting, just in case we ran out of dried meat. I dipped my hand into the satchel and grabbed a handful. Bozak looked on disapprovingly. He never approved of eating outside meal times.

I liked archery as a sport. My bow was nothing special, crafted out of wood, from a tree by some skilled bow makers at Hawks Nest. It was arched with an upper limb and a lower limb, and carved out in the middle was a neat sight window with which I could take aim and it was held together by a thin fiber cord. It was light and had proved more durable than I had expected, having dropped it on more than a few occasions.

Our journey would take us through Sarastria and through its capital where I had hoped to visit a temple dedicated to the Goddess Chandi, my other half. It was an ancient temple that had thus far withstood the test of time. According to most sources it was where the Goddess resided. My other half chucked, I could hear her. Well I guess that's what most people thought anyway. Who was I to say otherwise?

The weather grew warmer as we journeyed east and as we drifted farther away from Hawks Nest the landscape brightened up. It was a scenic journey and I watched the landscape change, dropping its snowy, barren, rocky facade to take on patches of greenery. Sarastria was a fertile state and much of the food that we purchased came from here. Therefore it was in our interest to ensure that the state fared well.

As we entered the state, I was warned to keep my sword out of side. The folks here didn't take too kindly to armed strangers riding into their territory unannounced which was exactly what we were doing. I replaced my sword with a string of rosaries. I probably played the part well, which was more than what I could say for my companion.

His posture gave too much away and he was having difficulty assuming the humble façade of a lowly monk, not to mention the large broadsword that he carried with him. It was difficult to hide, and was best kept in a sheath strapped to his side. We stopped for awhile to allow him time to make the necessary alterations to his persona. Finally, after minutes of unsuccessful tries we decided to camp for the day despite the early hour.

We set up tent well before sunset, by a narrow creek that was filled with cool, crisp, clear running water. I couldn't resist dipping my feet in and pulled it back out as soon as I did so. The water was unexpectedly cold, unlike the mountain pools which I had been used too. I couldn't help but wonder if the magic that held it all together had disappeared. "It had" was the uncalled for response in my head.

"Magic, depends on the people. In Hawks Nest everyone read the language of the Gods and recited mantras. The air was rife with magic". "As we drift away, the number of people who used the language and recited mantras gradually diminished and as a result the magic slowly disappeared". "Thanks, dear one" I replied. My other half had once again enlightened me as she so often did.

I sat by the creek while Bozak pitched the tent, something he was adept at. It looked a perfect camping site, a small spacious turf on one side and tall trees on the other with a small creek running in between. I didn't see the need for a tent, and I would have been perfectly comfortable sleeping on the thick moisture-less luscious green grass, but the orthodox soldier in my travelling companion insisted that we had our tent up and that we built a campfire to its rear. He appeared to have forgotten his troubles with his broadsword momentarily.

We started by collecting wood from the nearby forest that bordered the turf and soon we had enough wood for a bonfire. We piled the wood together in a heap, and set it alight. I walked to the creek to get some water which was several hundred yards away and as the flame got higher I could hear it crackling. I couldn't help but chuckle, Chandi did the same. The boyish side of the beloved general had got the better of him.

By the time I got back he had managed to get the fire in some semblance of order, and had put a kettle on, with corn oil gently simmering in it. I sat beside him and it made me hungry just to watch him cook. First he threw in chucks of meat from our supplies, which he had diced with a small knife. Then he threw in bits of potatoes, chopped onions, and some other dried vegetables that we had brought along with us. He didn't add too many spices and there was no need for additional salt because the meat was already salted. It was ready within minutes.

We brewed some coffee and dug in. I was famished and despite the lack of preparation or seasoning, the food tasted delicious. We ate to our hearts content and decided to pack away the remainder for breakfast the following morning. The sun had set by the time we were finished and we decided to get in an early night, leaving the fire to burn itself out.

We got up the next morning just before sunrise and after saying my prayers, I decided to brave the cold and jump into the creek nearby. The water was chilly but I needed a good wash. We had been on the saddle for days, and it took me ages to scrub off the dirt and grime that had accumulated all over my body in that time. Fortunately we were clad only in monks' robes and we had brought extras that allowed us to change regularly. Bozak jumped in soon after and once we had scrubbed ourselves clean we proceeded to do the same with all the clothes that we had gathered over the week or so that it took us to get here.

We waited until it was an hour past noon for the clothes to dry, feeding off the leftovers from yesterday, which surprisingly enough tasted much better, than that of the previous day. Maybe reheating had enriched the natural flavors in the food.

We headed for the temple which was located in the capital, Chandisha, named after the Goddess Chandi. On the way we passed small, neatly tilled farmstead, and homes with thatched roofs. I couldn't but help admire the scenery. It was a magical green and I wondered what it would have been like to have been born a normal boy and to have spent time playing in the fields with my friends.

"It wouldn't have been all that great, let me assure you" came the voice inside my head. I smiled and turned to look at the stolid, tight lipped man beside me, who rode without moving a single muscle. He must have seen me looking at him with the side of his eye. "It's pretty isn't it?" he asked. "Yes" I replied very much so. "It is one of the prettiest parts of the world. The weather is just nice and the people are friendly enough" he continued. "I grew up here you know" he said. That took me by surprise.

"Oh", I said, unsure what to say next. "Why did you leave?" I asked. "It wasn't for me, the farming; I was more the adventurous type". "I used to get into a lot of mischief and eventually my father tired of me and tossed me out of our home". It was sad, I thought. "What did you do?" "Well, I was too young to fend for myself and my friends had deserted me at the first sign of trouble".

"I walked around for awhile and tried to take on a job as a farmhand but I was no good at it, so I had to keep moving from place to place until I finally came across a monastery". "I knocked on its doors and the principle monk immediately realized that I was born with the talent". "He took me in and sent word to Hawks Nest, who were always on the lookout for boys and girls who were born with the talent in them". "I trained as a monk for many years, before I was sent to Hawks Nest to be trained as a warrior". "I worked my way up from there".

Talent is a word we used to describe children that are born with a closer nexus to the super soul than most. Because they are more in touch with the Brahmatma they are usually gifted with extra sensory perceptions like clairvoyance that most people just would not understand. Some of these children especially those with exceptional abilities have a difficult time growing up in the normal world that had lost its religious heritage.

Hawks Nest took in as many of these children as it possibly could and fined tuned and sharpened their skills. Eventually they became leaders in their chosen field. Many became warriors or those we called "warrior priests" but very few became leaders of sects. That distinction belonged to those who could not only transcend time but could usurp the karmic consequences of their actions and escape retribution.

We spent the night by the gravel track and pitched our tent in the bushes close by. We wanted to get an early start and the enemy was on both our minds. We spoke little of it but we knew our treasured way of life was in danger. Time had a strange way of forgetting the old and ushering in the new.

We got up the next morning before sunrise and we set off almost soon after that. We were on the road for weeks; we travelled at a slow pace. There wasn't any need to rush. We continued with our lessons in swords play as we progressed. I sometimes took the time to do a bit of archery, not that I killed anything, with the exception of a chip of wood. There was no need to; we had plenty of food in store. Occasionally we'd stop by an inn or a tavern for a cooked meal and to determine if there was any news of the enemy.

As far as we could tell nothing had happened in these parts, and to us it was a clear indication that the enemy hadn't yet ventured this far east. However we had no doubts that they would eventually do so and if their offensive wasn't checked it might culminate in a mammoth battle, the outcome of which was unpredictable at best. I remembered something I learnt in my lessons.

"Warfare is the art of deception. Therefore, if able, appear unable, if active, appear not active, if near, appear far, if far, appear near. If they have the advantage, entice them; if they are confused, take them, if they are substantial, prepare for them, if they are strong, avoid them, if they are angry, disturb them, if they are humble, make them haughty, if they are relaxed, toil them, if they are united, separate them. Attack when they are not prepared, go out to where they do not expect."

"Generally in warfare, keeping a nation intact is best, destroying a nation second best; keeping an army intact is best, destroying an army second best; keeping a battalion intact is best, destroying a battalion second best; keeping a company intact is best, destroying a company second best; keeping a squad intact is best, destroying a squad second best. Therefore, to gain a hundred victories in a hundred battles is not the highest excellence; to subjugate the enemies army without doing battle is the highest excellence".

The trip to Chandisha was uneventful but enjoyable. My companion and I had a chance to talk openly, something we had never done before and getting away from the strict routine of monastic life put a different perspective on things. We reached the temple just after dawn and we went around behind. We left the horses on a free reign so they could graze easily, and walked into the temple passing beggars who were pleading for alms.

As we walked in we bumped into a man and his young daughter. I walked straight into her. The young girl, who looked half my age, took a step back dazed and I was taken by surprise. I stood there looking at her unsure of what to say. "Sorry" popped into my head; the next thing I did was repeat my name. "Kathiresan" I said, without being asked. It was lame and I felt rather bashful but I didn't know what else to say.

The girl stared at me blankly for a second not knowing what to say before she replied "I'm Anamika". I could read kindness in her eyes. She turned her head towards her father before asking him, "Can we give the man some money?". Her father nodded his head and handed her a few coins. She motioned for me to hold out my palm with her hands and I obliged, too dazed to think. She tossed the coins in my hand and walked off with her father smiling. I was taken aback and I didn't know what to make of things.

I turned towards my companion who looked equally taken aback. Far away close to the foothills of the Gorgon Mountains another girl was sitting on her bed in a tent made of animal hide, laughing. My face turned red for a second, but there was nothing I could do. I put the coins in my pocket. I guess fortune was smiling my way. The old adage never look a gift horse in the mouth came to mind.

We walked into the main precinct of the temple and for the first time I caught a glimpse of the Goddess Chandi, in her omnipotent self, fair skinned and armed with a weapon in each hand. She was extremely pretty but her eyes were full of anger. I was instantly absorbed by the power she emanated. "Steady yourself little one" the voice in my head said.

I tried to make out the age of the statute but it looked infinitely old, maybe over a thousand years old and in all that time the statute and the idol in the main altar had been kept in good care. Beside the Goddess, I saw two lions on either side that looked so real that they could have come to life at any time. "My pets" was the answer to an unasked question.

We left the temple after saying our prayers, requesting for the aid of the beneficent and benevolent Goddess in what would no doubt prove to be testing times. We didn't move at a great speed, there was no need to hurry. The scenery remained picturesque and I had to admit the memory of Anamika kept slipping in and out of my mind, together with the occasional interjection by Chandi, the auspicious Goddess of War. If the truth be told, Chandi sometimes didn't look much like a War Goddess but more like a young girl with milk stains on the sides of her mouth and dress.

As we crossed over to Amestria which bordered Sarastria, I felt an eerie sensation creep over me. It was like someone was watching me. "The Sisterhood" said a little voice in my head. I turned to look at Bozak, who remained unmoved. It was not that someone was actually spying on me from a distance; it was the presence of a new form of magic that I was unused to that gave the sensation. It sometimes played more on the mind than on the body. It was the feeling of being in the presence of others and it was easy to pick up especially if one had fined tuned his or her instincts, which in my case were honed in from birth.

"So what is it" I whispered, when we got a chance to speak. Bozak shook his head "there is no need to whisper little one, it's not like anyone can hear you, in the middle of nowhere". I must admit I was a bit disappointed. Wasn't I important enough to be spied on? I heard a chuckle somewhere. I didn't bother saying anything. He probably didn't feel it or was acquainted with this type of magic.

Nothing looked out of the ordinary and people moved about as they normally did, at least I thought so anyway. They didn't look particularly bothered either. The task he said "was to locate the renegade Lamunian general, Triloka". He had become somewhat of a legend in a short span of time and when we started making inquiries, rumors were rife everywhere.

Some even when to the extent of calling him a God incarnate and in an isolate village they were in the process of building a temple to worship him. I shook my head in disbelieve. No doubt the man was a hero but elevating him to Godhood was overdoing things a bit, I thought. I made up my mind. If the enemy did not invade Lamunia I would, just to strengthen our grip on it. "Blasphemy" I thought to myself.

I pondered over it for a few minutes when it suddenly occurred to me that having another God on my side; even if it was one that was mortal could not hurt my cause. In fact it might unite the people. Nothing worked better than religious fervor.

I mentioned it briefly to Bozak and he nodded his head in agreement. We quickly decided that we would make a generous donation to the locals. With this in mind, we approached the villagers, and shared some of our food with them, which was always appreciated in these parts and gave them some gold coins to buy building materials for their project. They were no doubt pleased to meet other "loyal devotees" especially those who represented Hawks Nest.

I decided to take matters further and elevate Triloka's status by giving him his own set of mantras. I added the standard seed mantras to give the mantra the desired effect. Seed mantras are normally used to produce successful results. I gave it a bit more thought and decided that it might result in a positive outcome.

Despite my not so honorable intentions, Triloka meant the ruler of the three worlds and it is a word used is reference to the God Zhiva who is sometimes known as the mountain mendicant, the omniscient wielder of the trident. In addition to gaining their support there could be an additional twist in the right direction to this. I decided to take things a step further and elaborate on the mantra that I had just written. I had vivid images of creating a new series of sacred texts when the little voice in my head flashed another message and said "don't". "Spoilsport" I countered out aloud, forgetting briefly that I was in the midst of an endearing audience. Fortunately no one thought much of it and I continued.

"Laud Triloka the God of the five nations, he who is the past, the present and the future. May the god of equity, justice and fairness, great father of all that is good and noble, guide us lest we should falter and be led astray".

"May the beneficent God spread his wings wide and far, taking us in his fold, thereby bringing us under his protection and dispelling any evil that may befall us".

"May we ascend without sin the vessel of righteousness and row it with strong and steady arms. May the boat that never leaks despite any turbulence, despite the unsteady wind of change that may come our way sail smoothly on the endless ocean of creation. May he in whose lap the spacious air resides afford us the protection of the three layers. We sing in praise of Triloka, the loftiest of Gods, and seek his guidance and assistance in our endeavors".

"Let us go forward in search of glory and riches secure in the knowledge that divine Triloka will evermore be at our side. Benevolent Triloka, divine guardian of creation, we approach thee as son to father. May thee take us under your protection, never failing to intervene and intercede favorably on our behalf".

I wanted to continue but my traveling companion was giving me all sorts of looks, probably telling me that it was time to be on our merry way.

So I decided to wrap things up with a simple "peace to all'. My audience looked a bit disappointed but I assured them that I will bequeath them with more mantras on my way back and encouraged them to create their own hymns and verses in their native tongue.

A splintered nation was always easy prey and once again my mind revolved around Triloka. Nothing divided or united people more than religion and right now we needed a hero of such a stature. Triloka sounded exactly like the man we wanted. I discussed it with Bozak and he agreed. We needed to inject some religious fervor into our campaign.

As we continued our journey we spread the word about Triloka and hoped that the new warrior God that we had created would do the job. Over the next few weeks we started erecting altars for our new messiah in every rural village that we came across. Our coffers soon ran dry but there was plenty of gold in the monasteries. People were generous with donations especially when monks could perform miracles, which they did ever so often, with the help of Hawks Nest.

DHAYANAM V

"We are all born with the talent but it is evident more in those who are not preoccupied by the senses. The five senses are like intoxicants and they drown our wits in a pool of emotion. The sixth sense that is prevalent in those who are in touch with the fourth dimension is the only true sense" – Hawks Nest

As we rode further into Amestria, the landscape began to change and the terrain became increasingly rugged. There were no visible signs of fighting. War, I understood was not always fought on the battlefield. It is possible to force the enemy into submission without going into battle and there was no better way to do this than to cut off the food supply. I discussed it with Bozak. He nodded his head ruefully as he replied. "It is a time old strategy that has never failed, slow, ruthless and effective".

"It creates manifold problems especially for monarchial states". "Starvation often leads to rebellion and now instead of just fighting the external enemy, soldiers have to also content with the enemy within, and the conflict escalates into a two pronged war".

"A prudent enemy does exactly what our enemies are doing, they destabilize a nation, cause civil unrest and to cap things off, if they can provide the necessary supplies, especially food then they will be heralded as heroes".

"The control of food and other basic necessities is essential to victory. Adequate supply of basic necessities and raw materials or the lack of it determines the stability of any government. By controlling supply or exerting a monopoly on supply we have the ability to determine the future of any state" he continued.

"If we wish for the state to prosper then we ensure that enough supply is released into the market. Supply determines price, excess supply while it benefits consumers is detrimental to producers and retailers. Therefore we have to manipulate supply in a manner that ensures that all parties benefit".

"If we wished to disrupt an economy, all we need to do is to strangle supply thereby creating shortages which will inflate prices. Soaring prices leads to discontent among the masses which will manifest initially into minor protests that will eventually develop into major protests and riots if not addressed. To date supply is the most effective mechanism to disrupt any state or economy" he added.

"Do we keep adequate food supplies" I asked. Bozak nodded his head. "We have stores of access supplies not only in Hawks Nest but also in all our monasteries. To date it has been our most effective means of reaching the masses".

"Much of it has to do with economics. When we manage to improve the standard of living of any community their faith increases many times. Religion or any aspect of it is meant to increase the standard of living and not decrease it or diminish it in any way. Even as we speak our monks and their allies are busing themselves ferrying supplies to those who are afflicted by the swaying tide of battle". I understood.

The terrain slowly began to change. The lush green began to fade away and the trees along the mud beaten track grew further and wider apart, its leaves, spotting the odd intermittent, withering brown. The grass grew thinner and the air was humid. There was water, plenty of it, made visible by occasional flowing rivers that intersected our passage; shallow barriers that we crossed with ease.

The sky was a pale blue filled with soft cotton like clouds that sometimes looked a pure white. There were odd showers and rain came without warning but by then we had already developed a knack for riding in the rain.

The showers were initially short and mild but as we progressed further north it grew heavier and the journey was occasionally delayed by pouring incessant rain. The torrid showers hampered visibility, the water aided by gushing winds, got into our eyes. It dampened the soil and the tracks become muddy; the horses could not be pushed or urged. At times, the best we could muster was a gentle walk.

Despite the difficulties it was a pleasant trail, littered with scattered farms, and village homes made of thatched roofs and mud bricks, reinforced with dried cow dung. The nights were noisy, filled with the sounds of small insects and the loud chorus of crickets.

We soon reached another forested area. It stretched for miles around in all directions as far as the eye could see. It looked like it was centuries old filled with trees that reached hundreds of feet upwards.

We rode on for days before we reached another secluded village. It was an ancient land, a land of beauty, culture and wisdom. On the northern fringes of the village was a small settlement. It was a fertile area and many of the village dwellers were farmers who worked from dusk to dawn. There was plenty of water and sunshine and the ground was fresh with humus from rotting vegetation.

We saw small children playing, venturing into the forest to gather wild honey and fruits. It looked like the most popular time of the day for the children, who no doubt spent many glorious hours dwindling away in the shade of the trees. Watching them from a distance I instinctively felt like reaching for my hunting bow to do a spot of hunting.

I could hear the sound of running water and I heard the voices of children frolicking away in the sunshine, probably swimming and fishing, no doubt soaked to the skin. There was nothing more enjoyable than a swim in the river on a hot sunny day when the sun was at its peak.

The heat made the sweat pour down from Gavin's brow. No matter how many times he tried it he could never get used to it. He was a tall lad no older than sixteen, his skin a charred brown, a result of continuous exposure to extensive heat. It was a rich, fertile land but unknown to most, deep in the timbered forest; there were underground caverns with a wealth of untapped mineral deposits.

The best iron in the world came from the underground labyrinths deep within the Amestrian forest floor. Its vast mineral resources had led to the growth of the iron trade. Ironmongers and blacksmiths from far and near had set up shop to cash in on the plunder.

Traders came from all over the world to purchase iron wares, to fuel the wars that were erupting in the west. The war was growing bigger slowly spreading to the north and the east and the armies or warring factions needed to be furnished with weaponry.

They came from everywhere, traders, soldiers, and mercenaries; to this almost forgotten land to stock up on supplies. Over the years the craftsmen of the land had fined tuned their skills to produce the best metal works on the market.

Bronze in itself was brittle, and could never be depended upon during intense battle. Bronze swords broke easily, and the craftsmen of the land forged their weapons in iron to produce more durable weaponry that could withstand the stress of battle.

Despite his young age, Gavin was a master of his trade. He started when he was no older than nine, an orphan deserted in the streets to find his way in a merciless land. Fate had dealt him a cruel blow but here, he found kindness among the hardened ironworkers.

Their rough exterior hid a gentler nature and the men and women he met took pity on him. They fed him and gave him clothes to wear. The fittings were drab but that didn't really matter because most ironmongers wore drab garments anyway. In time he found a kind master, who took him in and taught him how to work a foundry and mold metal. The metal had to be cast and knocked under intense heat before it took shape.

The process would sometimes release noxious gases into the air, but the metal workers knew how to overcome the ill effects of their trade. There were certain herbs and plants that they cultivated that would neutralize the toxic effects of harmful gasses and dissolve any toxins stored in their bodies. The workers consumed these plants and herbs daily during their meals and it not only cleared their body of harmful toxins but also made them stronger and healthier.

Gavin mastered his trade in a short time, and was soon a top rated blacksmith. Fame had its rewards and his works fetched a high price. Weapons forged in his hands withstood the test of time and the young man worked tirelessly, day in and day out to perfect his skills.

It was during one of these routine days, that Bozak and I approached the young man with the feigned excuse of purchasing a new sword. The young man was hard at work and had his sights set firmly on the blazing flames that shaped the steel.

"Excuse me" said Bozak; the young man looked up, his pale blue eyes reflecting an aura that belonged only to a select few. Bozak took a step back. I recognized the symptoms instantly. He like us was blessed with the talent.

Bozak shifted gear immediately. "I'd like to purchase a sword" he said. The young man didn't give him a second look. "We have an array of swords at the back, forged from the best metal in the land" he said, mistaking us for either traders or soldiers. The robes that we had on didn't appear to make much of a difference to him. An attendant stepped up, a boy no older than ten and offered to lead us to the rear. "Is it possible to have a sword fashioned to our needs?" I asked. I didn't know where the question came from, it just popped into my head; my other half obviously had something to do with it. "What are your needs?" he asked curtly. My other half took over and by the time I had finished speaking Gavin's face went utterly pale. I was trembling at what I had just said, gapping in utter disbelieve and Bozak was visibly shaken.

"All…things are possible" he stammered. "But only someone who was blessed with the talent can fashion a sword like that which you seek" he continued.

"You are blessed with the talent more than you know and if you follow us, we will show you how to harness it". Gavin went silent and after some thinking he nodded his head in agreement. He didn't appear to need much convincing.

A day or two later, when we were camped in the forest, he opened up. "I always knew I had it in me" he said. "I inherited it from my mother. She had the ability to see the future, she tried to help people at first but eventually the villagers had her labeled as a witch and they expelled us from the village. We went into the forest for refuge and finally, after years of suffering, she died of heartbreak and misery" he said.

It was a sad story but not unlike many others that we had heard before. Many of those with the talent were misunderstood and often tormented. Some like Gavin's mother were tortured. Others were quartered, hanged and burnt at the stake.

People failed to realize that both white and black magic emanated from the same source. It is an inherent gift more transparent in some than in others and how it is utilized depended on the individual.

Despite his rough exterior, which lacked polish or refinement he had a gentle personality, soft and tender on the inside. He looked like he needed as much love and care as possible. Leadership I realized didn't always involve fighting wars. A good leader needed a gentler touch, the ability to care for his people and sometimes the ability to do so, had to be manifestly apparent. I had become so caught up in planning strategies and counter strategies that I had ignored the finer points of leadership.

We decided to head for Dashia to continue our search for Triloka and his men. It was a steep climb to Dashia which was a nation built on a plateau between the Quest Mountains and the Darya River. It was rugged and hilly, almost impossible to assail and I pondered on how it had fallen so quickly.

I asked Bozak. Dashia he said "was a nation that had splintered into many communal factions centuries ago and despite having a monarch it was governed by provisional and sectarian leaders who at times disagreed with the king". "When a nation is divided like Dashia the job is made much easier for the enemy".

A small armed contingent led by a vizer with a smooth tongue and a pouch of gold will be able to forge the right alliances". "War is not always won by means of a sword; in fact, battles are last on the list". "Remember, my most astute pupil, go only to battle when all else fails". It was no doubt good advice, given by someone who had witnessed many wars and secured many victories.

Gavin remained silent, he looked shy and the confidence that we saw when he was hammering way on molten metal was no longer there. I decided to bring him into the conversation. "You have seen many warriors in your time Gavin, what do you make of the whole situation" I inquired. He thought the question over, before he replied. I like the way he didn't gush out with his answer, but thought it was more appropriate to think before he replied. That was the trademark of a leader. Someone who is full of bluff or bluster would never last long and worse he would compromise not only his troops but also his nation.

"I have seen many traders and representatives make their way to my blacksmith's in recent times, attired in different styles, speaking in various accents and buying weapons. Sales had increased almost twenty fold in the last year and I think they anticipate a war or a demand for weapons in the near future" he answered.

Bozak smiled, "Quite astute" he said. I nodded my head in agreement. The road ahead proved more difficult than what we had expected and we pushed on at a slow pace. It was almost dusk when we reached a nearby village. Quiet and secluded on the foothills of a sizeable hill which looked tedious to climb. I was too tired to even attempt it and I was certain that my companions felt the same.

We decided to head for a nearby village instead. There were no clouds in the sky and a pale orange hue lingered in the air. There were small patches of grass on the ground and flowers were in full bloom. The petals were alive with ants and bees busing themselves with gathering nectar. A perpetual wind displaced all humidity, and the climate was mild to chilly. We decided to camp in the bushes close by, too tired to adopt an orthodox approach.

We drifted into sleep without fuss. Bozak's military ways had suddenly deserted him and even he began to see the merits of not pitching a tent when there was no need for it. We woke up the next day and made for the nearest village, just as the sun was about to rise.

As we drew closer to the town, we spotted a quaint monastery, painted with white from a limestone quarry, with a tiled roof, strengthened by concrete walls. We fastened the reins of our horses to the rails nearby and walked towards the front door.

Just as we were about to announce ourselves, I heard the voice of a young boy singing a hymn. He had a lovely voice and we couldn't help but listen in silence.

"Praise to Dawn who rides her silver chariot drawn by her solar steeds whose luster ushers in the morning sun and dispels all traces of the night. Praise to her who is most worthy of worship, her beams and her splendor, stretch from the heavens above to the ocean floor. Praise to the Goddess with the golden colored hair, of the four prettiest women in the world, she who is adorned with gold and silver, and garlanded with the glory of the morning.

Praise to the daughter of the heavens whose radiance dispels all doubt and whose brilliance disperses all fear. Like a valiant archer, like a swift warrior, she banishes any lingering traces of darkness.

She passes easily through the hills and the meadows and her light sparkles off the white waters of the oceans, glistening and glistering, blinding all that is evil, spreading instantly over vast distances.

Shedding her light on us she calls us forth from slumber. She brings hither the man who worships glory, power, might, food and vigor. Opulent in her manner she favors us like heroes favor their servants. Dawn who brings oblation and stands prominent on the mountain ridges, she who gives wealth to noble heroes, shine your light on us."

It was a hymn sung to one of the most worshiped Goddesses of the Empire, Dawn, she who ushers in the light of day and banishes any lingering traces of doubt and uncertainty. Her worship had almost faded away after the fall of the Empire and it was refreshing to find a monk who still remembered the old ways, the ways of the Empire, the ways of Gods and warriors.

They went hand in hand Gods and warriors. A warrior of the Empire never failed to worship his chosen God or Goddess. They worshiped might, they worshipped success, they worshipped power and they worshipped wealth. But above all they worshipped their Gods, without whom, success was never assured.

The sun was sneaking up behind us when the boy stopped. We knocked on the door and I heard the gentle ruffle of robes from within. Moments later, the wooden door swung open and in front of us looking rather uncertain was a young boy no older than twelve.

He recognized us as monks instantly, and clasped his hands together, bowing his head in respect. We did the same. Gavin, who wasn't yet well versed in our ways, stood rooted to the ground. "Greetings brother" said Bozak, taking the lead while the rest of us remained silent. "We come to seek refuge in you humble house of prayer, little one" he continued. The boy nodded his head, "follow me" he said sounding sterner that he looked. The façade of the austere monk didn't last too long. "Are you hungry?" he asked. I nodded my head, and his face betrayed signs of compassion. He was gifted with the talent. My other half sighed. "Another recruit" she said.

I smiled, "the more the merrier" I replied and I could hear the faint squeals of a suppressed giggle hundreds of miles away. He led us to a room at the back of the monastery. Inside there was a square dining table, with stools and makeshift chairs on all sides. It looked out of place in the white placid room, undoubtedly put together by the monks with their own hands but it looked like it suited its purpose well.

"Are you the only one here" I asked. He shook his head. The rest are in the backyard tending to the garden. "We have a large compound that we plant with crops. It adds to the food supply, which sometimes dwindles, during bad harvests". "How long have you been here" asked Gavin who was having a good look around as he spoke, unused to any surrounding that didn't include a blazing fire and molten metal. "I was orphaned here at birth" he said, and we all sympathized with the boy instantly. Children with the talent were often, ignored and disowned.

He walked into an adjoining room and soon returned with a bowl and loaves of bread. He sat the bowl on the table, and it was filled with a thick vegetable broth that had visible chunks of meat at the top. We were all famished and we dug in instantly, forgetting to thank our gracious host. It was only moments later when we had filled our bellies that I remembered the magical words. "Thank you" I said and my companions nodded their head in concurrence still engrossed with their meal.

"What is your name, little one" I asked. "Usan" he replied. "It's a lovely name". I heard the creak of a door somewhere and I could make out the audible sounds of footsteps, followed by talking voices, with traces of a strange accent that was unique to this part of the world.

The sound of walking feet grew louder, and the room was soon filled with monks who looked to be between the size of a full grown man and a dwarf clad in saffron robes. All of them had bald heads, customary to monks in this part of the world, years of hard labor visible on their faces, the lines and creases smoothed over by a cheery disposition.

"Who have we here" asked the chief monk in a booming voice that was filled with mirth while the others fell behind, in orderly fashion, looking to be in high if not good spirits. Usan quickly introduced us, hesitating when it came to our names, simply because we were so hungry that we overlooked the customary introductions.

Bozak stepped in at this stage and as the monks clambered around the table, he made the formal introductions. Soon we all became embroiled in a conversation. They wanted to know what's been happening in Hawks Nest and the conversation took a lively turn as we narrated the events that had transpired. Someone put the kettle on and soon the air was filled with the smell of brewing coffee, its aromatic scent, drifting all around the room.

The dwarf looking monk, whose name was Kalden, fished out mugs from a wooded cabinet in the adjoining kitchen and soon started handing mugs of hot coffee all around. He put a spoonful of chocolate into the mugs that he handed to Usan, Gavin and me. I was delighted; I had a sweet tooth and a special craving for chocolate, which were almost impossible to come by at Hawks Nest. It was a classic combo, coffee and chocolate and the mug that he handed to me tasted absolutely divine. It was the highlight of our journey so far, followed by finding Gavin and now Usan.

We spoke to the monks in length about Usan and convinced them to let him come with us. The monks treated him like a son, and found it difficult to let him go, which was understandable. I don't think I could part companies with my guardian either but they knew like the rest of us that it was for the best. The boy was gifted and with the proper training we could develop his talent.

It was impossible to ascertain the full potential of any child, gifted with the talent, and therefore each child was an untapped resource that was waiting to explode. The possibilities were endless.

In Hawks Nest we tried to bring anyone gifted with the talent closer to the Brahmatma and by doing so helped them realize the abilities that lay untapped within them. We not only schooled them but we nurtured them as well, regardless of their age. When we accepted a new recruit we cared for him or her like a child.

DHAYANAM VI

"The mourning period for the dead is no longer and no shorter than 365.2 days in which time the soul would have walked down the corridor between lives or would have attained salvation. Souls that haven't crossed over will linger on as spirits, sometimes helping, other times haunting and in extreme cases possessing" – Book of Souls.

Triloka surveyed the valley below sitting astride his stallion as the calm mid morning breeze bit through his leather mail. Unfazed his mind pondered over the events that had transpired in the recent months. The transformation that had come over him and his men was absolute. Hate he decided flamed the fuels of rage and it was the most lethal weapon in his arsenal.

He was a wise general, cold, calculated and ruthless when the situation demanded it, cunning when it was required, gentle and compassionate where possible. His attributes earned him the respect and loyalty of his men. His enemies despised him and wanted him dead by any means but the wily fox had thus far evaded capture and had brilliantly executed his plans. He knew he could not keep it up forever and eventually he would falter.

The sun slowly slipped away and night inched closer. The workers deserted their farms for their homes and the orchestral chorus of insects grew louder. The aging barn owl left its abode and silently perched itself on top of the branch of a tree, its saucer like eyes on the vigil for tiny rodents that would make a hearty meal.

Close by in the lush green forests the soft sounds of flapping bat wings could be heard leaving the cave that was their home during the day. Like the tree the bats were native to this part of the world and both had coexisted harmoniously for thousands of years.

Coexistence thought the general was something that men could learn from animals especially those that took to the air. Unlike humans who preyed on each other the winged ornithoids had little or no trouble living harmoniously with one another as they industriously labored to survive.

Wise were the ways of birds thought the general. Alas it was not for men. He surveyed the land below, his eyes taking in every minute detail. The towns and valleys were rife with rumors of a band of renegades who were brutally slaying members of the Serpentine Army.

The village folk were alert; their hearts filled with inbred pride, they sung praises of Triloka and his men and were eager to help when they could. It was troublesome and Triloka's biggest fear was that in their overwhelming desire to help, they might inadvertently betray his men. Loose tongues were as deadly as sharp swords. He waited the night out patiently like a lion on the prowl, silently stalking its prey, inching closer to the kill with each passing minute. Dawn was the most suitable time for attack, when the senses were not at their peak, the mind dulled from either sleep or the lack of it and the belly rumbled in hunger.

The enemy had camped beside a river in customary fashion, with a thin defensive perimeter comprising of a handful of guards who were as alert as well fed pythons. Serpents he decided were only a danger when they were hungry.

If caught off guard they were easy prey. Was it their conceitedness that made them that way? It was difficult to say. They were the exact opposite of their natural predator the hawk. The bird was constantly alert and its keen eyes never missed a beat.

The enemy had their backs to the river and had evidently ruled out the possibility of an attack from the rear. It was based on the common premise that an enemy on horseback clad in armor would not risk crossing the river. To some extent it was true, and if the tides were strong and the water was deep both man and animal could drown. Triloka however had structured his army in the mold of a light infantry that traveled with minimal armor and attacked in a flash. During the night he had his men crossed the river in little bamboo rafts held to together by strips of chords. Having crossed the river, his men silently took up their positions.

Dawn came with rosy fingers and the sun appeared over the horizon drawn by its chariot of solar steeds. It slowly climbed to the summit and the birds began to chirp in unison. The general watched as the men in the camp lumbered to get around, carelessly going about their daily tasks. The warmth of the Amestrian sun made the men sweat and they labored their way around. Dressed in leather and armor they were ill suited to the task and their bodies were soon dripping with sweat.

Triloka waited patiently, the hawk was looking for the right moment to strike, and if fortune favored him, the sizzling heat would have his enemies on their knees and they would be right for the picking. They planned to attack when the men were most vulnerable, when they had their minds on their bellies. The smell of cooking food soon filled the air and the smoke from the lighted fires could be spotted from miles away. His men were signaling him and the hour of death for the enemy would soon be at hand. Triloka thought back willfully, it was months since he and his men had managed a warm meal.

They waited hidden in the bushes, silently watching as the men gathered around the fire, in line, plates in hand, as the cook dished out handfuls of stew. The men huddled together in little groups relishing their meal, famished by the long tiresome ride. Most soldiers never looked forward to the prospect of war. It was too precarious and the tide of battle could never be accurately predicted or anticipated. Even the most formidable contingent faced an element of risk and was subject to shifting fortunes.

Today was one such day and despite the skill that was abundantly evident in the manner the men carried themselves, it would be of no avail. Today they were destined to meet their doom in the hands of a more lethal enemy. Triloka gave the signal for his men to attack and within seconds the soldiers were pelted by a rain of flighted arrows. There was no escape and the slightest scar from the poisoned arrowheads would prove deadly.

Like trained soldiers those that were not too grievously wounded stood to face an enemy that never presented itself but chose instead to hide within clumps of bushes and behind trees waiting for the last possible moment when the soldiers, battered and bruised, by repeated showers of arrows were at their weakest. They spared not a single man and the final stroke came when the soldiers were weakened by the poisoned tips.

Triloka's men waited until the soldiers faltered and then with a blood chilling war cry rushed at them from all directions, sword in hand, and cut them down without hesitation. Thinning the enemy was the object and therefore no one was spared. Victory was theirs with minimum casualties. They piled the corpses together and set the heap of bodies alight before riding off disappearing once again from whence they had come.

"Finding the general might be more difficult that one would anticipate" said Usan, in his normal monk like manner. Apart from the ability to state the obvious the boy had a knack for sounding like a well written book which no doubt came from years of living in a monastery. It was annoying at times. He appeared to have almost no sense of humor but I liked him.

He was filled with stolid old fashioned common sense that was rarely found in most people. It was a commodity that was abundant in Hawks Nest. Gavin on the other hand may need a bit of work or maybe a lot of work.

It was almost a week since we had left the monastery with the new additions to the team and in that time they had little success in locating the whereabouts of the general. He was as elusive as a magician at the local bazaar and as slippery as an eel, but there were tell tale signs everywhere. They were getting close but Triloka was a man who didn't want to be found and given his ability to blend in, it could be months before they caught up with him.

It was then that the blacksmith hit on a plan. "Why not let him come to us" he said. I must admit the plan had his merits but I doubted that a veteran and three lads would be of much interest to the renegade general. Without doubt we needed a proper unit and after much deliberation we hit on the plan to hire some locals to play the part. We needed a troupe of actors and we decided to make inquires in the next village.

We passed a couple of small villages, sparsely populated that didn't look like they offered much in the way of entertainment. The third village that we came across was much bigger with homes and buildings that looked like they belonged to merchants and other small businesses. It was exactly the type of town that we were looking for. As per the norm, we looked for the monastery which was normally located along the main street. We found it without too much difficulty.

The High Priest, larger monasteries usually had an internal hierarchy, was a fat burly man, with beady eyes, his face smooth and clean-shaven. I instantly disliked the man; I sensed greed and an unsavory pervasion. As we entered there was a strong smell of incense in the air and I got the whiff of lime that was normally used as a detergent, to not only remove strong stains but to also eradicate persistent scents and odors that could not be displaced by more conventional methods.

What could cause such a stench I wondered and the little voice inside my head said "sacrifice". Of course the smell of death and rotting carcasses would leave a stench so putrid that it was impossible to discard. It was pungent, permeating and heavy. There is a distinct odor to death; I recognized it from the piles of corpses that I had confronted. The stench was disguised, covered by perfumes that were toxic to the body. I felt nauseous and was on the verge of throwing up. I looked around and I could see the look of disdain on the faces of my companions. My belly churned and I tried desperately to hold down my meal. It was an unpleasant odor much more intense than the rotting and decaying flesh of dead animals and infinitely more acute than that of rotting eggs.

The monk looked surprised to see us and bowed his head, finding it difficult to bend over. It was meant to look like an act of extreme reverence but unfortunately it came out as superficial. I was instantly suspicious and I was certain my companions felt the same way. He smiled, his mouth betraying a set of yellow teeth, visible stains of excessive smoking clearly evident. It was otherwise a perfect row of teeth set in place without blemish.

"Welcome dear monks" he greeted, his voice high pitched and squeaky. He gave the blacksmith a disapproving look and Gavin returned his gaze with a glinty stare. The monk feigned surprise, placing his hands across the mouth. I took another look at him, still trying to hold down my lunch, trying to hide the contempt on my face.

"Ritualistic sacrifice" said the voice in my head again. Chandi my beloved friend was giving me an advance warning, her tones menacing. I could feel the anger in her voice like a distant rumble. Come my brothers he said leading the way.

Unlike most monasteries this did not resemble a normal house or an abbey. It was an old monastery that had been rebuilt. Held together by arched stone pillars that separated the floor from the roof, painted with winged serpents and demonic depictions that belonged in the realm of folklore.

I was certain however that they did exist; all things are possible to those who are connected to the abyss.

There were a couple of attendants who scurried around as we entered. They looked too preoccupied to take any notice of us. The High Priest clapped his hands and the attendants stopped what they were doing and promptly approached him. He was about to speak, when our general politely beckoned to the High Priest that he and Gavin had to step out. The High Priest grudgingly gave his approval but I don't think Bozak cared too much. The blacksmith gave him a surprised look and followed behind.

He left Usan and me in the company of the High Priest. The man rubbed his hands together and affixed us with a brotherly stare that looked more deceiving than convincing. His skin had a sickly hue that sent shudders down my spine. It reminded me of an animal stalking its prey, but even animals don't prey on their own cubs. It was a repulsive thought.

We stood there for well over ten minutes and while the High Priest was gleaming, his powdered body, reflected a pale sickly hue that was to say the least unbecoming and looked out of place even for a professional dance troupe. That brought my mind back to the task at hand. We needed to find if they were any acting schools around. With that in mind I decided to make some inquiries holding back the abhorrence.

I asked the robed man with a beaming facade if he knew of any troupes that were for hire. He looked surprised at first, "I didn't know Hawks Nest was interested in our local artists" he said, but that soon turned into a broad grin, as he began to explain the nuances of the local artistic community.

It was a lengthy explanation and as he started to elaborate, his narrative became lively and his arms began to move in all directions as he described the performances of the local entertainers. He even went to the extent of regurgitating lines from local plays. His portrayal were extremely boring, to say the least. We stood there pretending to be taken in by the grand performance that was on display, patiently waiting for the men to return. Fortunately we didn't have to wait too long and once they returned, the High Priest showed us the way to our quarters.

There was no doubt that the High Priest was gifted with the talent but his was pervasive, and tilted towards the darker aspect, common among those who were more preoccupied by the senses. Not all children with the talent are born the same; some are born with an acute sixth sense and are more in touch with their sub conscious mind. These were the children that belong to Hawks Nest.

Others were born with a strong desire to fulfill their sensual needs and these are the children that were most likely to slip into the dark side and become preoccupied by satisfying sensual pleasures or desires. The High Priest was a prime example of one such child.

They were gifted like us and could do the same things we could. The powers of the universe were unlimited and anyone connected to the fourth dimension was able to tap into these powers. Power required discipline, absolute power tended to corrupt absolutely and corruption went higher than the need to acquire money or authority. It was a sickness that played on the mind and there was a constant desire to acquire more.

"How many people live here" asked the general, his voice calm and collected, with a menacing edge that would have escaped most people but I knew him well enough to detect the subtle changes. "I would like to meet them all" said the general. The High Priest paused momentarily, before he answered. "I'll summon them" he agreed, after a minute or two of deliberation. He didn't look too pleased and like everyone else who was blessed with the talent he could tell when there were signs of danger.

He told the attendants who were waiting silently close by to summon the others. The attendants scurried off to all corners in search of the missing monks and minutes passed by before the evasive monks appeared. The general looked them over. They were unpleasing to the eye sullen and burly and like the High Priest. They showed signs of excessive meat consumption.

The general looked like he was about to speak, his eyelids closing slightly and the corners of his mouth spread wider. The little gestures had everyone expecting a speech of some sort when as quick as lightning he pushed his robe aside and in one swift movement drew out his sword which was hidden beneath the loose fitting robe and lashed out with it at the High Priest, severing his jugular veins in a single stroke.

The High Priest clasped his hands around his throat to stop the blood from flowing but it was too late, the life blood was oozing from his throat. The remaining monks tried to react but unarmed they were easy prey for Gavin, who like the monk had a sword strapped neatly beneath the shirt on his back. He drew it out and coldly stabbed at the belly of the monk closest to him. It was an untrained stroke but one look with the naked eye would tell anyone that the blacksmith had used the sword before and was not averse to a fight.

The remaining monk and attendants tried to flee but the general and Gavin chased them down in quick time and made easy prey of them. The gleaming floor was soon stained with pools of blood but it didn't look like it was the first time that it had happened.

I was certain that the High Priest and his band of vagabonds were engaged in the practice of ritualistic sacrifice invoking the dark Gods of the abyss and the elixir of life was the nectar that the evils from the world below demanded in returned for the favors they conferred on those who required their assistance.

I must admit that I didn't feel any remorse at the deaths of the men and I was surprised that the general failed to hide the tinge of sadness that appeared in his eyes without warning. Gavin sat down on a chair close by looking drained, the effort, regardless of the victory had sapped his bodily energy. The rush of adrenalin during battle often left one feeling numb after it dissolved. I looked at the carnage around me and felt a sense of relieve, evil I said to myself had been vanquished. My other half agreed.

I pondered for a minute on the lack of remorse and I decided that I despised beyond measure all evil and I could never feel remotely sorry for what I perceived and understood as evil. I never made a mistake, not when it came to demons. I knew them too well; I had fought countless battles in countless lives with them. It was then that I achieved cognizance. Our enemies were being manipulated by demons and the invaders were merely vassals who had inadvertently opened the door to the abyss and what came from beyond had taken complete control of them.

For them there was no turning back. All things had their time, even demons and the age of the demons was looming large on the horizon. Battles would be fought on a mammoth scale with weapons that could destroy planets. I had a sudden glimpse into the future and I could see worlds being torn apart as the conflict spiraled. The continued preservation of the sect was paramount for without them all would be lost. "Let us inspect the rooms" said the general. I followed lagging behind as the company went through room by room. Each room appeared to be neatly furnished but despite the measures that had been taken to make the interior of the rooms pleasing to the eye, the smell of death and decay lingered in the air. Old, stale and musty, it had attached itself to the walls.

I continued to follow behind and towards the end of a long corridor; we reached a flight of stairs that led towards the basement. I followed the men down a long spiraling staircase and as we progressed downwards the pungent repugnant stench grew increasingly stronger. I could see smudges of blood on the walls and I had no doubts in my mind that we were heading for a dungeon of sorts where prisoners were interned. Human sacrifices were performed here under the influence of drugs and other intoxicants.

It was not the first time I had heard of it. The walls were made of cobblestone with moss growing from splintered crevices. Chains were attached to the walls and shackles were hammered to the ground. The cells differed in size, each complete with corrugated iron bars that kept the prisoners within. We saw children of various ages, girls and boys un-kept and untidy.

Lined neatly beside the walls were urns and jars the size of full grown child and only then did it dawn on me that once the children were sacrificed, the remains were put in urns and jars before being buried. "The sacrificial chamber is located further within" said the general. He turned around and asked us, "Do you want to see it?" he asked. I gulped. Usan shook his head while Gavin remained silent. I nodded my head. I was suddenly overcome by a feeling of extreme sadness. It was inhuman to subject these children to the type of suffering that they had been subjected to but these men had lost their humanity a long time ago. For those that had brutally perished we had to perform their last rites.

**

There are forty prescribed rites or passages from birth to death but as individuals we do not participate in two, first that which is performed from conception to birth and second that which is performed after death. The distinguishing factor that determines if the soul remains or lingers as a spirit or migrates to the next body, physical or astral, rests in the performance of the last rites. The prescribed mourning period is one year during which various ceremonies are performed to ensure that the soul of the deceased is at peace and follows the natural sequence towards the attainment of salvation.

If the death rites are not performed in accordance with the requirements or are performed inaccurately or callously, the souls of the deceased will not be appeased and the dead will return as ghosts, specters or haunting spirits. They will continue to remain thus until the final rites are performed in accordance with custom.

The mourning period of one year is a distressful time for the soul and the relatives. The spirit will linger around its loved ones, and family members may often experience hints that the spirit remains in the vicinity. It is up to them to complete their duties and fulfill the requirements in accordance with tradition.

On the sixteenth day following the death an offering of food is made to the deceased. A lump of flour mixed with water is flattened on a tray and left beside the food. It is not uncommon to see imprints of a hand or a foot on the flour the following morning. The death rites for those who had died a timely death and for those who had died as a result of accidents, murders and suicides are slightly different. Suicide is strictly forbidden and it is a sin to take one's own life.

Those people who kill themselves and others willfully will enter a world of blinding darkness. After experiencing the tortures of a thousand hells, they will be reborn as a village pig. Nothing auspicious will befall those who kill themselves and others without cause or reason, either here in this world or in other worlds.

Those who die through suicide are counted among great sinners. Such sinners do not deserve a burial by fire. Similarly rites performed by sinners bear no fruit. For those who die by suicide there is no rite of cremation, no water-libation, no rite of obsequy or impurity.

The customary requirements were difficult to fulfill because the duties begin immediately after death. Under the present circumstances we could only take the time of death as when we discovered the remains. Immediately after death, custom requires that for ten days without intermission, the relative or a loved one or the person that has assumed the responsibility of mourning for the departed should offer rice balls and pour handfuls of water in favor of the deceased.

The rice balls are divided daily into four separate parts. Two parts go to the building of a new body. The third part goes to the messengers of the God of Death, Maya, and the fourth part the deceased consumes himself.

DHAYANAM VII

"Upon death the soul travels to the Kingdom of Death, dragged by a noose around its head and there it is adjudged by the Death God. It is either suitably rewarded or punished depending on its deeds while it was alive. Once it has enjoyed its guerdon or repented for its sins, it walks down a long corridor with doors to the left and to the right" – Book of Souls.

With the first feed the head is formed; with the second the neck and shoulders; with the third the heart; with the fourth the back; with the fifth the navel; with the sixth and seventh the waist and private parts, with the eight the thighs, with the ninth the palate and with the tenth the deceased acquires pangs of hunger. On the eleventh and twelfth day, the soul eats to his fill.

On the thirteenth day the soul begins its journey towards the city of the dead. The soul is captured by the emissaries of Maya, who are armed with nooses. The hangman's halter is slung around the neck of the unfortunate soul and it is led on its journey, its neck constantly tugged at. The journey takes a year and at the end of the year the soul reaches the dreaded City of the Dead. Here it gives up its dreadful body, and acquires a new body befitting its karma, before it moves on to the corridor with doors on both sides to step into a new life.

The soul carries with the burdens of the sins that it had committed during its lifetime. There is no way to cleanse the soul of the sin prior to death and the only way to do so is to undergo the punishment prescribed in the Book of Souls. The atonement is severe and it is beyond anything the mortal body can accept or endure.

In cases of unclaimed bodies, where the death rites have not been performed for the deceased, the souls will wonder the earth until the preordained or predestined time of death. At the appointed time of death all souls have a choice to either cross over or to remain. Those that remain are the spirits that linger.

These are the souls responsible for hauntings and possessions. At the time of death most spirits are reluctant to leave the material world and the spirits that make the smoothest transitions belong to those who have no interest in material wealth or possessions or are without familial ties, usually belonging to hermits and sages. It is the longing that binds the soul to the material world.

For those who have committed suicide or for those that have died an untimely death, daily prayers and offerings will have to be performed for a period of one year. Offering of food served for all those who participate in the rite will have to be cooked outside the house. Under no circumstance, for that period, must anything remotely relating to anyone that has died in the aforesaid manner be brought into the house.

Once the year is complete, the affectionate descendents should do the following. They should worship the God of Death on the eleventh day of the bright half of the month with incense, flowers, uncooked rice and offer rice balls soaked in ghee and mixed with honey and gingerly seed.

Those who die an untimely death also derive satisfaction through the rice balls are that are offered. This includes all those who have committed suicide, those that have fallen in battle or succumbed to accidents and those whose deaths were self inflicted. Fasting to death however is not considered suicide. For those whose souls had been darkened by the touch of malice they would be subject to immense suffering before they can be freed again.

Bound by its past indiscretions the departed soul is brought before the Death God Maya, to be adjudged and adjudicated. The soul is hungry and thirsty and between the time of death and until the time it crosses over, it is in need of sustenance.

The distance between the point of death and the court of Maya is three hundred and sixth five point two days long. During the journey the soul is bound by its misdeeds and dragged by the emissaries of the death God with a noose around its neck. The soul passes sixteen cities before it finally reaches its destination.

The righteous comply and the sinful resist. The pain is excruciating for the latter. The consciousness remains and the soul seeks desperately to return to its former life of comfort, luxury and in the case of the High Priest, a life of extreme pervasion. It is relevant to differentiate between souls that have died at the appointed time and souls that die before the predestined hour. The emissaries of Maya appear like clockwork at the time of death and not before. Reprieve can only be granted by the Brahmatma.

When the sinful soul first crosses over, it is drained and sapped, its remains devoid of water but there is not a drop in sight. It feels the blistering heat of twelve suns beat relentless down on it. As it moves further inwards it is struck by a sordid wind, cold and remorseless, that blows at the rate of knots and carries with sharp thorns that pierce its decaying and decomposing sin.

It screams in anguish from pain and terrifying cold, as frost bites into its limbs. As it walks its feet are stung by venomous snakes and scorpions, before eventually passing through a jungle, filled with leaves as sharp as a razor's edge. It is repeatedly bitten by the most venomous animals. Vultures peck away at it and hawks swoop down from the skies above, sinking their claw into the flesh.

It faces every type of pain it had feared, and avoided during its lifetime and refused to subject its body to. The consciousness lingers and refuses to depart. When it reaches midway, it arrives at the shores of the River of Tears, which inspires sorrow and fear in all men. Thus is the ego subdued and pride becomes naught.

The journey continues for seventeen days and on the eighteenth day it reaches a new city, the City of Jewels. It is a beautiful city of untold splendor, rich and divine, decorated with gems of immeasurable value. The residents of this city live in grandeur. The corrupted soul, lost and destitute laments the loss of its wealth and its possessions.

It is here that the emissaries of Maya say to the desperate soul, you suffer as a result of your own sins. It is you actions during your lifetime that have brought about your suffering. Those who have fulfilled their duties and have acquitted themselves honorably need not to suffer, for they die in peace.

The soul then journeys to the Kingdom of Pain and there it is brought before its king, Agarva, who wears the face of death, and his eyes speak of infinite horrors. Upon completion the soul travels to the City of Terror, the city of dark and unyielding forests. During the whole journey, the soul feeds on offerings placed at the altar by its next of kin, who continue with the death rites as required by custom, tradition and religion. At the end of the second month the afflicted soul leaves that city.

In the third month the soul reaches the City of Sand and on the fourth month it moves on to the City of Stones, where it is pelted by hails of stone, falling relentlessly from the sky, each the size of a man's fist. Still feeding off the offerings made by family and relatives, the destitute soul longs to return to its former life, while the emissaries of Maya scorn and mock in contempt.

In the following month the soul travels to the City of Sin and from there it goes to the City of Misery. Towards the end of the fifth month, before the beginning of the sixth, a ceremony is performed by the family and relatives of the departed.

The soul is somewhat happy, the first chance it has had to be so, after relentlessly being tormented by the emissaries of Maya. Trembling and miserable, lost and forlorn it continues its journey. The city of misery is ruled by Zarga, the younger brother of Maya, who resembles in size, a demon of gigantic proportions. The soul is instantly intimidated at the sight of Zarga. It shrieks and cowers in fright and in a feeble voice begs for mercy and clemency.

The soul runs in fright to the banks of the River of Sorrow, and there it greeted by boatmen who are willing to grant it safe passage across the river if it is deemed worthy. For the soul that has accrued merits by performing acts of kindness and compassion, passage is granted and for the soul that hasn't, it is left to drown, nibbled at continuously, as parts of it decayed and decomposed body are torn off in small bits by a multitude of sharp fanged creatures that lurk beneath the murky and muddied waters of the rivers.

The emissaries of Maya affix a skewer that pierces the lips of the soul and it is dragged across the river by his emissaries, who take to the air, towing the soul across, by the lip. It suffers immeasurable pain. When it reaches the other side, it is famished, and feeds off the offerings made by family and relatives. At the start of the seventh month the soul approaches the City of Solitude. Here it is left, in peaceful silence, to ponder, reflect on its sins and savor the offerings of food and other items made by its sons and daughters, lamenting the loss of all material wealth and possessions.

The soul having contemplated the life that it has led departs for the City of Despair, traveling in the air like a flighted bird; it is stung repeatedly by winged insects and cries out in pain. At the end of the ninth month the soul travels to the City of Anguish, filled with the noise of a thousand wailing souls. The faint hearted soul sinks deeper into desolation as the loud and audible laments fill its ears. In the tenth month threatened by the emissaries of Maya the soul goes to the City of Desolation.

At the completion of the eleventh month it journeys to the City of Respite. Here once again the soul is able to enjoy the offerings made by its sons and daughters. After a fortnight it is taken by force, dragged by a hangman's noose around its neck to the City of Storms. Here the dark cloud gathers and it rains without stop. Thunder and lightning pound the unfortunate soul and a year passes after the death of the soul. Here it benefits from the homage paid to it by its living relatives. The year complete it journeys to the City of Ice, a hundred times colder than the summit of the highest mountain. Frost bites into every nook and cranny.

Hungry and forlorn with cold winds piercing the decayed body in all directions, the soul confused and perplexed looks everywhere for hiatus. Finding none it leaves for the City of Fallaway. Here the decomposed body finally falls away revealing the soul, a light, the size of a thumb. The soul takes to the air with the messengers of Maya, to the abode of the king of death, who presides over the City of Death. The City of Maya has four gateways, each facing a separate direction. The southern gateway is allotted to sinful souls.

It is this singular light, the soul that forms the essence of the body. Without it the body is nothing but an empty shell and it endures long after the body has ceased to exist. In cases of hauntings or possessions, it is normal to hear accounts of sightings of small orbs of light moving in specific directions. The light is normally white but spirits that are malicious, or seek to hurt or harm others often appear in circular lights the shade of black.

Understanding the dualistic nature of existence is essential. The soul, the little light that exists within the body, is that which is commonly referred to as the subconscious or the super consciousness. It transcends time and space and any illness of the mind or body can be cured by addressing the grievances of the soul. It is this little voice in the head that is the progenitor of intuition and premonition. Understanding the mechanics of this little light paves the way to a higher existence.

At the time of death, the first stage is that of the transition; than that of repentance, then at the end of the year, after the walk along the long corridor, reincarnation. The soul without the body is like a flame without fire. It is about the size of a thumb. After leaving the earthly body, the soul obtains an airy body. If the body is fed with food and drink, what then is the soul fed with?

All things alive require some form of sustenance, and the soul is very much alive, more so than the body, and while the body requires rest and gradually deteriorates with age, the soul remains the same, constantly alert, unburdened by the passage of time. The soul is fed with good deeds and positive energy that is derived from charitable acts. Even the humblest of men, those who exist in the lowest strata of existence, often shunned and ignored by the status quo derive some form of satisfaction from helping others.

When the soul enters the City of the Dead it is greeted by the doorkeeper, the ever vigilant, Dharmad. The door keeper reports to Maya's minister in chief, Sharad, who tallies the merits of the soul in accordance to the deeds it has performed during its lifetime and submits a synopsis to Maya.

The King of Death asks Sharad, of his sins, and the all knowing Sharad, despite knowing the truth, consults the sons of the creator Sravan, the Sravanis, as dictated by tradition. The Sravanis have the ability to travel as fleet as the wind through existence ascending to the highest heavens and descending to the depths of the netherworld and therefore are all knowing and all seeing. They report all things to Sharad, as do their wives on all the activities of women, with the utmost discretion, unknown to anyone.

Bound at birth to speak only the truth, the all seeing Sravanis, tell of the virtues and vices of the soul, to Sharad. To the soul that has lived its life, with truth, honor and kindness, never failing to perform charitable deeds, they are benevolent. To the wicked and sinful, they dispense misery. Holy and pious people see Maya as a God of noble countenance, while the sinful and the wicked see him as a God of dreadful and terrible aspect.

Maya, having assured himself of the sins and vices of the soul summons it, seated on his buffalo, staff in hand, longer in length than the height of a full grown man, his eye the burning red of a thousand funeral pyres, glares at the offending soul. When it appears before him, he roars like a lion, his voice as ominous as the sound of a thousand thunders.

Having seen him the wretched soul cowers in fright, its mortal body no longer. "Know this, sinful soul, Maya, deals with all manner of men and women, the rich and poor, beggars and interlopers" says the God of Death. Upon hearing those words, the soul remains silent and resigns itself to its fate.

The sinful soul is then sent to the first precinct of hell. The tortured soul cries out in anguish. This however is only the first precinct. There are in total eight million four hundred thousand precincts of hell of which twenty one are classified as the most dreadful of the dreadful.

The soul is tormented by all manner of tortures conceivable and the unrepentant soul is continuously subjected to it. For those who haven't or cannot disengage from the sins of mortal life, their memories linger painfully in their consciousness, like an unrepentant scar, and nags away in their thoughts. As directed by the King of the Netherworld, the sinner after completing the punishment in hell is reborn in the lower species of animals.

The characteristic features of those who have had their hardships in hell and are reborn include scandalizing others, ingratitude, outraging the limits of decency, ruthlessness, cruelty, attachment to vices, stealing, blasphemy, harassing, deceiving others and miserliness.

As for the virtuous, splendid aerial cars arrive, decorated with sweet smelling garlands to take them to heaven. When its merits are exhausted, the virtuous soul falls from heaven and is reborn in the house of kings or nobles of illustrious character where it enjoys various pleasures.

There is one manner in which all men can escape the court of Maya. If one makes daily offerings and worships his chosen God or Goddess with sincerity and gratitude, Maya does not see such a man or woman and neither do his emissaries. Nor does such a man or woman see the torturers in the regions of Maya.

The characteristic features of those who have had a happy stay in heaven and are reborn include sympathy towards all living beings, pleasant conversation, belief in a supreme religion, helping others, truthfulness, wholesome advice to others, belief in the authority of the religious order, devotion to preceptors, angels, celestial beings, divine sages, association with good men and women, eagerness in performing noble deeds and friendship.

I smiled gratified as my recollections from the Book of Souls came gushing back to my head. The High Priest no doubt, will feel excruciating pain. I uttered a prayer to the mighty Eryr to make it so. I was not at all ashamed of my lack of compassion. If the truth be told I never felt any, not for those who had so brutally committed the atrocities like that which was plainly evident in front of me.

What of the spirits of those that had been brutally slain to benefit the minions of hell? They might not make the journey to the underworld but unless their last rites are performed these souls will continue to linger in the vicinity of their death or close to their loved ones. The easiest way to coax the spirits into making the transition is by performing the last rites in accordance with religious principles.

I knew I had a mammoth task ahead but I wasn't sure how to go about it. I decided to ask my other half and the reply came instantly. Chandi was always dependable under these circumstances and could provide answers without a minutes thought. The bodies would have to be recovered from the urns they were buried in and each would have to be cremated in accordance with customs and traditions.

We entered the dark desolate room which was the sacrificial chamber. There was a large square table in the middle of the room, equipped with utensils and hooks. The slaughter or sacrifices of higher sanctity is done at the north side of the altar and it included the slaughtering of humans, bullocks and male goats. The reception of the blood is performed on the day of the half moon and the full moon with service vessels in the north. Their blood requires sprinkling between the staves of the ark, on the veil and on the golden altar. The residue of the blood is poured on the western base of the outer altar. Sacrifice if performed with a single stroke to the base of the neck which severs the head from the body.

Public and private sacrifices were performed in this room. The victims were slaughtered on the day of the full moon and their blood required the four applications of the four horns, one horn for each direction on the compass.

Once the sacrifice was complete the decapitated bodies were stuffed into the urns and taken to the backyard where they were buried. We followed the trail out to the back. It was not too difficult because there were bloodstains on the floor that led the way. In the meantime there were a dozen children in the cells drugged and shackled. Opium derived from the opium poppy and alcohol was used to sedate the children.

The children were incarcerated for a minimum of six to eight weeks and in that time they were left either in a stupor or rendered unconscious. Most would have lost their sanity and to bring them back to the world of the living was an almost impossible task.

There was nothing we could do for them at this stage, so we left them temporarily in their cells and decided to come back to them once we had located the remains of the dead children. The trail led to a backyard that was freshly laid in with grass and an assortment of greeneries.

There were intermittent barren patches and the topsoil had been churned over repeatedly, it looked fresh and un-broken. We knew instantly that this was where recent bodies had been buried but we could never be certain. We realized that in order to exhume all the bodies that were piled in the backyard we needed to dig up every inch of dirt. It was beyond us and we needed help.

We sent Bozak out to request for help from the local garrison and a request from Hawks Nest was never refused. Soon we had soldiers digging up every inch of dirt. Within the next couple of days we had uncovered almost a hundred bodies, buried over the last couple of years, many were well preserved because the monks had managed to drain the air from the urns before filling it with the remains of the decapitated children.

An incarnation carries with the burdens of the sins that have been committed in the previous life and the sin had to be cleansed if not during this lifetime then after death or the next life. There is a way to cleanse the soul of the sin prior to death and that is to undergone the punishment prescribed in the Book of Souls. The atonement is severe and it is beyond anything the mortal body can perform or accept. The souls or spirits belonging to those that have died prior to their predestined or preordained time or those that choose not to cross the threshold are the souls that linger and the souls that are responsible for hauntings and possessions. At the time of their departure most spirits are reluctant to leave the material world and the spirits that make the smoothest transitions belong to those who have no interest in material wealth or possessions or are without familial ties, usually belonging to hermits and sages. It is the longing that binds the soul to the material world.

It took us almost a week to exhume the bodies and in that time the men at the garrison had turned the vacant space behind the obscure monastery inside out. The urns were not buried in any specific manner and it looked like over time the bodies were buried one on top of the other.

Some of the urns had cracked under the impact of spades and shovels and putting the remains back into the compact urns proved to be a gruesome task. Once the urns had been retrieved, we decided that the best course of action would be to perform a mass funeral. There were over a hundred urns belonging to many different children, most of who we suspected were orphans and runaways that no one would miss.

They'd make the easiest prey and at a tender age they could be coerced into doing almost anything. Most orphans in these parts never survived beyond the age of twenty one. Gavin and Usan were among the fortunate ones who had managed to find reasonable if not comfortable homes.

We decided to employ a family, someone we could trust to complete the year long mourning ritual which was compulsory. After a year, if the mourners strictly complied with the requirements in the Book of Souls, the soul would be free and would be reincarnated as humans and elevated to higher or a better station in life than the one they had had.

As for the High Priest, I was certain that after a year of intense torture he would be reincarnated as a pig. The thought of him made me shudder.

We still had a dozen or so children that we needed to find homes for. We sent word to Hawks Nest requesting for the required potions and remedies to clear the effects of opium and to return them to sanity if possible but that would be a time consuming task. We placed the children in the care of another monastery that abided by the teachings of the sects and hoped that by the following year the children would be back to normal.

DHAYANAM VIII

"She looked up to see the sun slowly fading away, its brightness gradually hidden, covered by dark clouds that approached with the southerly wind. It made her shudder as she thought of the tales that she had heard. The southerly wind brought with it the spirits of the dead……..it is an ill omen…….the gate to the abyss had been opened" – Chronicles of the General.

The events that transpired had put us off our original plan of looking for a dance troupe and after almost a fortnight of exhuming bodies, and finding suitable accommodation for the remaining children, we had almost forgotten our initially task and that was to seek out the renegade general. In that time we stayed at a local tavern.

It was like many other taverns in these parts. It had several small rooms on the upper floor and one large room on the main or ground floor that was partitioned into separate areas or smaller rooms. The smaller rooms were formal areas where lady travelers could rest and taprooms where ale and cider were served. The larger room located at the front of the tavern and was used as the main dining room.

It was filled with a mixture of small and large tables; it had a fireplace and several comfortable chairs around it. The tavern's sleeping quarters were located upstairs. The kitchen was located, at the rear of the ground floor, where cooks served up hot sizzling meals usually of meat and an assortment of vegetables.

Behind the tavern, there was an outhouse or a backhouse and often a stable where travelers could rest their horses. There was a bartender who tended to the taprooms and in addition to ale and cider; he also served up local firebrands, various types of ale that were peculiar to the region. This particular tavern was clean and not overly crowded at any time of day. The owner - bartender was a pleasant man who served up healthy portions of ale while his wife did the same from the kitchen.

The lady was a fantastic cook. The food was served up with cider, which had a deviously sweet taste that was almost irresistible. It was only a day later, with a heavy head that I realized that cider packed a meaner punch than ale, and lying there my head in a daze, I forgot at least temporarily about our troubles.

Cider was in reality, as I was told later, fermented apple juice produced from apples that were too ripe to sell. According to the bartender these apples sometimes included fruit worms which gave the beverage a meaner punch. It had a sweet, pungent, vinegary odor to it which made it all the more enticing.

Fortunately the meals were not as deceiving as the cider and we were server with chunks of mutton friend in a blend of wild herbs together with potatoes and various other vegetables. It tasted scrumptiously good and despite the horrors we had witnessed, the cider increased our appetite and we had no problems downing our meals.

The men from the local garrison sometimes joined us. With the exception of the odd sentence or greeting they remained visibly horrified by what they had witnessed and it was plainly evident that they were unwilling or unable to talk about it. Time I hoped would heal all wounds but most of these men were scarred for life.

The innkeeper's wife served up another delightful meal, sizzling lamb chops, deep fried in fresh butter churned out daily in a small barn twenty or more paces away to the rear of the main building, with baked potatoes and melting cheese on top together with a pot of hot home brewed coffee.

I was famished and so were the others. Bozak never hesitated to dive into his meal and Usan said his customary prayers before attempting to carve away at the meat with his knife and fork. I was famished but despite that I decided it was time to make inquiries.

"Is there a dance troupe in town" I asked. The inn keeper's wife looked puzzled for a minute before she replied. "I didn't know you were into the arts dear monk" she replied. "We take an interest in all our flock" I said trying to sound as monk like as possible. Helga smiled; she was a jolly sort of person of average height and slightly plump around the waist.

"There is a troupe quartered close to the edge of town, in the third house from the end of the street". I nodded my head in acknowledgement and thanked our lovely hostess. After breakfast we decided to go in search of the troupe. According to the innkeeper's wife, who was very knowledgeable in these matters, they acted out all sorts of plays and were especially good at those that involved military campaigns of the past. The major military campaign in Dashia was almost a thousand years ago, so they must have good records. I ran it by Bozak.

"Most of the records" he said "are preserved through oral tradition". "Storytellers hand the story down from father to son, and the records, in most cases are conserved in his manner". "It is rare to find libraries in smaller towns but that however does not mean that there are no written records available" he continued. "Events of the past are stored both orally and in written texts". "I'll wager that there is a story teller in the troupe" he added.

It made sense. Not everyone knew how to write and plays were directed not only by scripts but also by oral instructions. Actors had to have not only a good memory but they also had to be diverse enough to be able to improvise when the situation demanded it. "They should be a fairly versatile lot" I continued.

We rode out and soon reached the building that housed the dance troupe. It was a large building and I gathered that the bottom floor was the stage and the top floor housed the living quarters of the actors. It was painted pink and purple with glitter and other bits added to the side, which clearly spelt out "artists live here". The vibrant colors were all the advertisement the troupe needed. It was impossible to mistake the building for anything other than what it was.

I jumped off my horse, leaving it loose and the others followed behind, the blacksmith and the monk at the rear. The main stage entrance that was located at the front of the building remained shut. It was almost nine in the morning but I guess actors stayed in late. "They are probably still in bed" said Bozak echoing my thoughts. "Plays normally go on until the early hours of the morning" he continued. I had never seen a play before so I couldn't say but it made sense. Performances were only put on after working hours, so the workers could come in. It didn't make any sense having shows in the middle of the day when most of the townsfolk were at work.

I walked up to a set of twin doors that were bolted from the inside and pounded my fist against the doors as hard as I could. If I expected an instant response I was sorely mistaken. I stood there banging on the door for a good ten minutes before a feeble voice from within called out. The man sounded like he had just woken up from a stupor. "Hold your horses" he yelled out feebly, his speech slurred, and a couple of minutes later, the door swung open to reveal a portly man slightly taller than a dwarf, his glimmering bald head, reflecting the light of the morning sun. "What do you want boy" he asked, obviously unable to distinguish between a monk and a normal person. I cleared my throat, "I'd like to see the owner of the establishment" I said politely.

The man stood there glaring at me wavering back and forth like a dancer swaying to the beat of drums. I must admit I found him rather amusing. I was about to say something, when Bozak walked up beside me, and callously pushed aside his robes unearthing a blade that was almost the height of the man at the door.

The man took a step back, "come in" he said. He turned and led the way. We entered the room that was moderately decorated, with three rows of uneven chairs placed between two aisles that led to a stage that was set with a red backdrop. The stage was divided into the left wing and the right wing which were aligned parallel with rows of chairs and there was a stage left and a stage right exit. The floor was littered with waste leftover from the previous day. It was still early in the day and the occupants after what was most likely a late night were still probably resting.

"Is he awake" I asked the dwarf like man, "the stage master I mean" I continued, who appeared to be in no hurry as he showed us the way. The light came flooding in through the open doors to unveil a set of Romanesque walls on either side that looked like they were badly in need of a new coat of paint. The red-bricked walls were common in this part of the world because of the many quarries. Laboring in the brick and granite quarries was the primary source of income for the townsfolk.

The walls had been plastered and painted over with limestone white, which I must admit, went well with the ruby red backdrop. To the right exit of the stage there was a wooden door that looked like it was made of oak but a closer inspection would determine that the door was made of teak and had been polished to refinement.

The man looked at the golden door knob as if it was about to jump out and bite him, before leisurely turning it and on the other side we saw a large group of people, seated around a long square table, in no particular fashion, having what appeared to be a morning meal, the sleep still evident on their faces.

Most hadn't yet fully come to their senses. I made a mental note to start avoiding these early morning starts. Not everyone lived in a monastery and got up before sunrise. He pointed to man wearing a white shirt, common in these parts, and a pair of black pants made up of a rough material which was dyed over.

He had black shinning hair, which was most likely oiled and appeared neat when it was combed. He was tall, slim and lanky unlike the portly dwarf who looked like he had jumped out of a fairytale.

Beside him sat a young girl and I felt a familiar sensation creep into my body as soon as I saw her. She was blessed with the talent but unlike most children that were blessed with the talent, who did not fare too well in life simply because their abilities were not recognized; she looked to have had a good start.

Like the stage master she was tall, and slim, and beside her was a large bow that was almost half her size. The bow caught my eye instantly and despite being a novice at the art, I fancied my chances against anyone. She turned to look at me and I realized she could sense my thoughts.

It was not uncommon and like Chandi's messages it flashed into the mind without warning. Some call it premonition or cognition. It sometimes meant the same thing. I let Bozak do the talking; a young man never really got much attention. I was a skinny lad and my bright yellow robes made me look even more like a child. I remembered the little incident at the temple, where the little girl Anamika had throw me a few coppers and smiled. Chandi giggled from nowhere. I resigned.

Bozak walked over to the stage keeper who courteously stood up from his wooden chair to greet him. Despite his disheveled hair, he appeared to be a gentleman but most actors and stage players are. Those that are learned in any field, I realized are cultured. That also sometimes applied to those who were unlearned. It was those who were neither here nor there that labored under false pretenses.

Bozak inquired if the troupe had any pressing engagements for the following fortnight, we anticipated that it would take us almost two weeks to flush out the renegade. If it was longer we decided we'd pay the troupe for as long as it took to make him come to us.

The plan was to tell the stage master whose name by the way was Mikhail which I thought it was a name that suited the stage master well that we needed at least a hundred actors to perform for a religious ceremony that was being organized by Hawks Nest. We planned to reenact a battle that had taken place almost a decade ago.

It was not something that was unheard of; religious battles were accepted as part of religious festivities. In the north the reenactment of these battles almost always included animal sacrifices that embodied or represented the slaying of demons. The carcasses were then cooked and fed to the poor to remind everyone that the karmic sin of killing can be mitigated by feeding the unfortunate.

The stage master was honest enough to admit that his shows were not getting much of an audience and that he was looking for a means of addition income. We made him a handsome offer and further gave him the assurance that all his expanses including the fitting of the outfits and the props will be borne by us. The stage master looked pleased. It was more than what he could have hoped for. We might be leading the troupe to an early grave but we decided to omit that minor detail. I was certain that we would be able to avoid any unfortunate turn of fate.

Over the next week or so we were busy fitting the troupe. Gavin was given the duty of filling the armory and we rented a forge for the blacksmith. He was delighted to be hammering away in the midst of a blustering fire again. I gave him instructions to ensure that the girl who sat beside the stage master, whose name I learnt later was Karmina, be given the best weapons possible. I had a feeling that she would be returning with us to Hawks Nest after our venture.

The armoring progressed without any hiccups and by the end of the week we were ready to move. Bozak briefed the actors on their roles. To make up the numbers we hired additional actors, who were more than grateful for the extra wages. We fitted them with black outfits, and the outlandish emblem of the winged serpents was attached to their outfits.

During the ride I had a chance to learn more about Karmina. She lost her mother at a young age. Her father never remarried and they lived in their little cottage. He was a farmer who worked and labored daily on the sizeable land they owned, sowing crops, and tilling the land with the help of a pair of water buffaloes that pulled the plough, helping loosen the soil so that seeds could be strewn and scattered in tidy rows. It was tough work, hard and demanding and it continued from dusk to dawn. Her father sometimes hired men from the local village to help him spread the seeds. While he worked young Karmina was left in the care of his sister.

Once the sowing period was over, he would be more relaxed with time to spare and he spent it in the company of his daughter. She reminded him of his wife and she resembled her in every way, imitating her features to the last detail. She had her dark brown hair, a pointed nose, and her hazel eyes were always watchful, constantly looking, always learning.

He was a good man her father, a soldier who had turned farmer, after sustaining injuries that prevented him from serving any longer in the king's army. He was rewarded for his years of faithful and loyal service with a plot of land that they called home.

He taught her how to choose the right type of wood, how to season it, oil it and care for it. She learnt to choose the right type of string for her bow, setting the tension to her comfort and make arrows with metal heads and how to select the right feathers for the correct trajectory. By the age of sixteen the young girl had mastered the skill of archery, her keen eyes and strong arms allowed her to hit targets at greater distances than her father could manage. Her tall slender body gave her the ability to move with the ease of a bird in flight and the speed of a spirited gazelle.

After her sixteenth birthday war threatened the once peaceful kingdom, and the frail old king who wits had been dulled by age and whose wisdom had been compromised by time, was no match for the onslaught of a superior army led by generals who were much younger and many times more able. One by one the villages fell, razed to the ground, its possessions seized and its inhabitants enslaved. Soon the invaders reached Karmina's village and after a brief struggle the villagers yielded. Her father was killed in the battle brutally cut down by horsemen. When the frontline comprising of local villagers faltered, a threat was posed to the archers - a common conundrum, for archers were secure for only as long as the frontlines held.

Karmina fled into the forest, it was the first time she had witnessed the savagery of battle and the shock lingered in her body for days after she had fled the scene. She rode deep into the jungle on her farm horse which was unused to traveling great distances and soon buckled under the exertion. She jumped off her horse with haste, setting the animal free and ran further into the thick jungle, in search of escape and salvation. The shock and panic in her limbs urged her forward until she finally collapsed from sheer exhaustion. Just as her body sagged to the ground the stage master found her.

We decided that she should ride beside Bozak, so we promoted her to the rank of lieutenant and relegated the stage master to that of a sergeant. He didn't look too pleased at the appointment but we assured him that the role of the lieutenant was merely a decoy and the role of the sergeant required more character. In our story, the sergeant eventually won the battle and was promoted to the rank of colonel.

After some persuasion and part payment in gold, the stage keeper readily agreed. Horses were another problem and we had to scour for horses from various farms in the valley. We tried to avoid farm breeds, which were the most common types of horses available. They were unsuited to battle conditions. It took us some time to acquire the right horses for our "soldiers" and additional pack horses to carry the supplies.

We were ready in a fortnight, Gavin was helpful but Usan had yet to make the transition from monk to warrior. The same however could be said for Gavin who had to make the transition from blacksmith to warrior and monk At least Usan was halfway there. We shed our priestly robes and after months on the saddle, I put on my leather armor. As I did so I could feel power, infinite power surge through my veins and a thought flashed into my head, "the warrior priest" is back, it said. I smiled. Indeed, I was back.

I understood that it was merely a contingent of actors that were riding into the wind in search of the renegade general but despite that I had difficulty in holding down the excitement at the prospect of a good battle. There was an inexplicable rush within me. In the months that I had been away there was a subtle change that had taken place in me and the priest within was slowly being shadowed by the warrior.

We rode for days, in the open, in two columns, towards the last sighting of Triloka. We made no attempt to hide our tracks, we wanted to be spotted and we wanted to draw the general to us. We observed the strict routine of a moving army and broke for camp at regular intervals, pitching our tents in accordance with established military guidelines. We didn't want to raise any suspicions and the general would certainly not attack if he was even remotely uncertain.

It was in the afternoon of the fourth day that I began feeling the strange sensation of being watched. I think some of the others felt it too especially those who were blessed with the talent. I had Usan keep a close watch on Karmina and the archeress got increasingly fidgety with her bow as the journey progressed. She kept looking left and right, trying to spot the watchers who without doubt were in the service of Triloka. I felt the excitement rise in tempo and my heart was beating increasingly faster, almost keeping pace with the leisurely beat of horse shoes trampling on the ground.

We moved at a slow pace, the troupe were not all trained soldiers or riders and to push them any faster would lead to the collapse of the columns. They had trouble keeping in line but were getting better by the day. Our meals were fun, in addition to good food; we also had the odd performance and song during our breaks. I must admit it was entertaining and it took my mind off things.

The food was well prepared, most of the troupe had some culinary skills and that enhanced our meals. Unfortunately they insisted on taking their time to get it ready and we normally had to wait at least an hour before we got fed.

The feeling of being watched grew increasingly stronger by the day, but I did not sense anything sinister. I think the renegade general was in two minds as to whether to attack or not. He was too wise and too experienced a general not to spot anything amiss. He needed some urging. That night while the others were sleeping, Bozak and I with the help of Gavin went on a little hunting expedition.

It was almost midnight when we set out. We knew the scouts would be close by but would station themselves far enough to make a quick getaway if they were spotted. We moved silently, careful not to tread on anything that might betray our presence. My heartbeat went up yet another notch, racing as it always did during the final moments in anticipation of what was about to come. Sword in hand, the dim light of the waning moon glancing off of the cold callous metal of my blade, I moved forward.

As we walked we placed the sole of our feet on the ground first and gradually brought down the rest of the foot feeling for any objects that might make a sudden noise as we did so. We walked in single file and half an hour into our journey we heard a slight noise.

He was close by and we encircled the scout who must have had a long day because he had let his guard down. It could have cost him dearly under normal circumstances but today he was fated to live. I could see him. He was nodding off. He had most probably decided to get some sleep while the rest of us, as he perceived, were doing the same. I waited for the appointed signal, the inconspicuous hoot of an owl and sheathed my sword in disappointment. There was obviously no fighting to be done. The hilt of my sword felt warm and welcoming in my palm. I was tempted to reach for it again.

Before I realized it I heard a hoot and without a moment's hesitation jumped like the others on our victim. The man was splattered to the ground and within the blink of an eye we had manage to gag and bind him, without giving him the opportunity to let out as much as a tiny squeal.

We dragged him bound and gagged as silently as possible. I had my foot on his back the whole time, just to make sure he didn't get a new wind of courage that would make him do something foolhardy and eventually lead to his death. It took us twice the time to get back and an hour or so later we were in camp. We decided to keep our prisoner flat on the ground until sunup. I relented an hour or so later and decided to lift my foot off his back. The poor scout looked buggered as it was.

The next morning at sunup we had the man in an upright position, sitting by the fire in plain view. The explanation that we concocted was that he was a thief who had snuck in during the night and we had captured him. I'm not sure that if the explanation made sense to anyone but if it didn't no one said anything, except to offer the man some food.

We saddled up after breakfast, I still couldn't shake off the feeling of being watched and kept riding on northwards. As we moved I spotted the odd deflection of light that I gathered were messages that were being sent from one scout to another. We rode at a more leisurely pace than normal;

the prisoner was made to ride in the middle of the column so it would be difficult to get to him. I desperately wanted to prevent an ambush so I remained as alert as possible. The general's men were deadly and I had no doubts in my mind that the troupe would buckle under the first wave.

We continued to ride until lunch without the slightest interruption. At the stroke of noon, we camped by a river, and those who were responsible for preparing the meal, we delegated the tasks, got cracking. Different groups were responsible for preparing our meals on different days. The actors didn't seem to mind. They all appeared to have a knack for cooking.

I sat around in the shade close to a clump of bushes, the prisoner next to me, with Bozak on the other side. The sun was high and I was feeling drowsy. I heard the silent rattle of branches behind me and suddenly a second or two later, realization hit me. I turned reaching for my sword but it was too later. There was a loud thwack and I went limp.

I wasn't sure how long I had been out for but when I awoke, the sun had disappeared and stars filled the sky. I looked up to see Bozak beside me. Standing next to him was a tall and sturdy man clad in mail shirt, his arms bare. The pale moonlight revealed a brown tan that came from countless hours of exposure to the sun. The sunlight turned the skin of a pale man to that of bronze God. I needed no introduction; I could tell that it was the renegade general Triloka. My head was sore, and I reached over to give it a gentle rub. "Sorry" he said softly.

I lifted my hand to say it was okay, I was still reeling from the shock. I made a mental note to always be alert. No doubt it was easier said than done. I looked around; we were in a camp surrounded by soldiers. One look at them told me that they were battled hardened veterans. They were clad in leather and metal armor, with sheathed long swords strapped to their waists or to their backs. Some had smaller daggers neatly tucked away in their boots.

What happened I asked Bozak when I came around to speaking, "We were about to be flattened but fortunately the general recognized the symbol of the Hawks Nest embellished on our swords. The mighty had Eryr intervened in a timely manner. I was hoping that I had managed to reach out to him with the talent but I guess I was mistaken. He must have read my mind, "and I sensed your good intentions" continued Triloka. That cheered me up a bit.

We disbanded the troupe and paid them off for their help. The stage master was a bit upset and insisted that we could continue with the play despite our repeated assurances that he and his company had performed their part in more than an admirable manner and that we had to return to Hawks Nest because of other pressing matters.

We had persuaded the renegade general to return with us to our unassailable fortress, together with the latest addition to the group the archeress Karmina. We rode back together until we reached town whereupon we waved each other a fond farewell after one last meal at the more than hospitable tavern, we journeyed home.

PROLOGUE

"The sun is the father, the moon is the mother and the earth is the belly in which all alchemic substances reside. The elements gravel, wind, fire, water and aether are that which give subsistence to the science of alchemy" – The Alchemic Sisterhood.

In the years that followed the new recruits were given the training they required to become what we dubbed warrior priests. They were born with the talent, it was within them and we helped them hone in on their skills and fined tuned their abilities to help them attain the highest levels.

It was a bitter, wintery cold morning when we rode out that day. I was in the company of Bozak, Triloka and Gavin; I had to visit Chandi again. Outside soft snowflakes were falling down like rain. Despite the warm fur coat that I had on my blood had turned to ice. It was time for me to acquire my battle sword. The sword of a warrior is never what it seems. A warrior relies on his sword during battle and should the sword falter the warrior is doomed. Thus one can only achieve the status of a true warrior once he has successfully completed the making of his sword. A warrior's sword is never merely a piece of metal forged in the flames of a blacksmith's fire.

It is often infused with charms and spells, designed to strengthen it in times of combat and to withstand bludgeoning impacts that are delivered during battle which is beyond the ability of undulated metal. Bronze and iron had to be worked with magic and forged with spells before either could be deemed fit to be beaten, cast and molded to become a warrior's sword.

The practice of strengthening weaponry with magic is common especially in the alchemic schools where base metal is transformed into other metals. This often involves the use of magic and the use of spells. Warriors whose armor and weaponry are strengthened through transmutation are often well versed in magic.

Metal is also transformed through the use of sound and vibrations. This is done by warriors who are well versed in chants and the correct pronunciation brings about the desired effect. By continuously subjecting the metal to sacred sounds the composition of the metal is transformed.

Then there are also those whose weaponry is gifted to them by others who exist on a different plane. The nature of the weaponry often depends upon the entities that are called upon and the weaponry can either be good or evil dependent on the forces that gifted the weapons.

Regardless of the manner in which the warrior gains his weapons he can only become a full fledged warrior once this requirement is complete. Once the warrior starts using the weapon he has acquired his personal characteristics change. Some will become the most noble of persons while others will become savage and brutal.

The snow had piled up by the time we reached the encampment and it was white as far as the eye could see. Horses were penned together with other domesticated animals that made up the nomadic livestock. Most of them knew us so we entered freely, unhindered.

I looked for the white witch's camp. She was the camp medicine woman and her tent had clear markings that couldn't be missed. I sensed my other half waiting inside. I rode up to it slowly, leaving the others waiting. "It shouldn't take too long" I told them.

None of them replied and they obeyed without question. I reached the tent, in a matter of seconds, and jumped off my horse. I walked over to the entrance and pushed aside the flap with my hand. I saw Chandi and the white witch waiting for me on the inside. The witch looked the same as I had always remembered her. She never appeared to have aged and as for Chandi, she looked lovelier that ever.

She was dressed in flowing white silken robes. She was no older than twenty one with long jet black hair, her skin the white of pearl. Her eyes a deep blue and her lips as red and as soft as the petals of a rose.

She was seated on a bed, her hair tied together behind her head in a single knot. I smiled and she smiled in return. We never spoke; she was always in my head. I nodded my head to say it was time. "She is ready" said the white witch.

I thanked her and she bowed humbly as was her way of showing respect. I reached out with my hand and Chandi took it. I lead her out of the tent and walked for almost an hour, her hand in mine, until we reached a lonely secluded spot. I turned around and hugged her; I couldn't stop the tears from trickling down my face. I held her close to me, her head in my shoulder.

While we were in a silent embrace, I reached for a small dagger that I had hidden at the back. I drew the blade out and stabbed her between the ribs. It was a lethal thrust and I could feel the warm blood from her body flowing on to my hands. She went limp and slowly sagged to the ground. "Now we are truly together" those were her last words. I waited until the last breathe left her body and carried her to the banks of a river. I cut away her hair, and put in a satchel that I had strapped across my shoulder.

I performed her last rites in accordance with customs and waited until the remains were reduced to a pile of ashes. I collected every bit of ash that remained and put it in an urn that I had brought with me.

I walked back to the rest and climbed on my horse. We rode home to Hawks Nest. Chandi was physically with me now. When we returned, my guardian greeted me, waiting for me as she always did.

I handed her the satchel and gave Gavin the task of forging a new blade. Once it was complete I attached the strands of Chandi's hair to the hilt the sword, at the top. I attached the hair to the hilt with a needle and thread. The stitching could only be undone by someone who knew the relevant spell and there were only two people in the world who knew it, my guardian and me. The ashes I mixed in a glass of water and in the presence of the Goddess, after reciting the relevant mantras I drank it down. It was done and now we were one, as it was in the beginning and as it will be in the end.

Soon after I began receiving isolated news that Sarastria had come under attack. I swung into action and started leading little forays, leading small units into battle. I took prisoners at first but I began to tire of the overwhelming numbers. In time, like Triloka before me, I executed them.

Even then I still managed to maintain some semblance of sanity but as they days continued I began to develop a lust for battle, more and more, I'd get myself into the thick of action and one eventful day, overcome by a passion that I could not explain, I rode out with a small company. Reckless and throwing caution to the wind, momentarily deprived of sanity, I allowed myself, to be caught off guard.

It was almost sundown. We were on our way back to Hawks Nest after a successful foray when we were attacked by horsemen from all sides. We fought tenaciously but overwhelmed by superior numbers and tired from a long ride, we relented and gradually we fell one by one. It was the first time I had tasted defeat. I fought valiantly but I was cut in the back. It was deep. I continued to battle on but as the blood began to ooze out of my body my knees started to buckle and my arms grew weary. Tired I let my guard down and someone stabbed a sword in my gut.

When he pulled it out I fell to the ground and I lay there feeling the life drain from body. The sky turned a blood red, I heard hoof beats, the riders were moving away. I looked up and over the horizon, I saw her, Chandi dressed in red satin, unlike the girl I knew. Her hair was disheveled, her face flushed with anger and her eyes burning with passion. She lifted me with her bare hands from the battlefield and took me aside, walking over the shattered bodies that lay scattered all over the ground.

I went limp, I had lost too much blood but she took me aside and as my soul was about to leave my body, she breathed life into me. "Not yet, dear one" she said. I lay there for hours. The sun had left the sky when I opened my eyes again. I was alive, and well, dressed in the yellow robes of a monk, a horse beside me, saddled. I felt strong again. I looked around and all I could see were bodies all around me, carcasses now, food for the vultures. I jumped on my horse and rode back.

I thought about the Chandi I saw and her voice flashed into my head again, "It was me dear one, that was the side of me that you have never seen before". I understood. She was the most exalted of all the warrior Goddesses, rarely worshipped and even then only by the purest and the noblest. She existed in tandem with the highest member of the sect.

I returned to Hawks Nest and my guardian was there to greet me as per the norm. She looked at me and at first glance I could tell that she knew what had happened. "You have been granted another life" she whispered softly. I nodded my head. "It was not yet time for you to die" she continued. I said nothing.

We had a quiet meal that night. Bozak and Triloka joined us. The mood was somber, silence filled the air. "How is she" I asked. "Who?" asked the general? "Anamika" I replied in an even tone. "She is well" he replied "but her lands aren't" he continued. I looked up, "what's wrong?" I asked. "They are under siege" he added. I thought thinks over for a moment. Having been granted a second life knocked the wind out of me for a bit. I sat back and gathered my thoughts.

In the months to come, the war took on savage twist. No longer were there isolated attacks and as we had anticipated it had festered into a full blown campaign on all fronts. Amestria, Dashia and Lamunia were the scene of bitter fighting. In the years that followed, I kept a close watch on Anamika, she became my ward.

Sarastria had become inundated with enemies and I decided on a change of tactics. I ordered the closing of all monasteries and ordered the monks, priests and anyone blessed with the talent back to Hawks Nest. Maybe it was the fact that I had been granted a second life but I did not fear death and I decided no else should either.

The enemy needed to sustain its army and it needed food. With this in mind I decreed that all farmlands should be set alight. Perceptions mattered and therefore I ordered that my men dress as the enemy, in order to win public support and drive them against the winged serpents. I intended to starve the enemy, death by starvation, as brutal as it seemed, was an option that I was willing to explore. Thousands died and the battle raged fueled by passion and ambition.